Also by M. C. Beaton
in Large Print:

Agatha Raisin and the Witch of Wyckhadden
Agatha Raisin and the Potted Gardener
Agatha Raisin and the Vicious Vet
Agatha Raisin and the Quiche of Death
Death of a Glutton
Death of a Prankster
Death of a Snob
Death of a Hussy
Death of a Perfect Wife
Death of an Outsider
Death of a Cad
Death of a Gossip

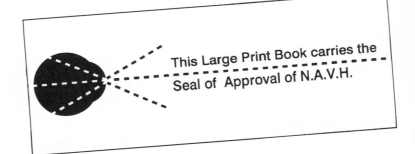

This Large Print Book carries the
Seal of Approval of N.A.V.H.

AGATHA RAISIN AND THE FAIRIES OF FRYFAM

✝

M. C. BEATON

Thorndike Press • Thorndike, Maine

Published in 2000 by arrangement with St. Martin's Press, LLC

Thorndike Press Large Print Mystery Series.

The tree indicium is a trademark of Thorndike Press.

The text of this Large Print edition is unabridged.
Other aspects of the book may vary from the original edition.

Set in 16 pt. Plantin by PerfecType.

Printed in the United States on permanent paper.

Library of Congress Cataloging-in-Publication Data

Beaton, M. C.
    Agatha Raisin and the fairies of Fryfam / M.C. Beaton.
      p.   cm.
    ISBN 0-7862-2858-X (lg. print : hc : alk. paper)
    1. Raisin, Agatha (Fictitious character) — Fiction.
    2. Women detectives — England — Norfolk — Fiction.
    3. Norfolk (England) — Fiction. 4. Fairies — Fiction.
    5. Large type books. I. Title.
    PR6052.E196 A66 2000b
    823′.914—dc21   00-062875

To Rose Mary and Tony Peters
of Fort Lauderdale with love

ONE

✝

Agatha Raisin was selling up and leaving Carsely for good.

Or rather, that had been the plan.

She had already rented a cottage in the village of Fryfam in Norfolk. She had rented blind. She neither knew the village or anywhere else in Norfolk. A fortune-teller had told her that her destiny lay in Norfolk. Her next-door neighbour, the love of her life, James Lacey, had departed without saying goodbye and so she had decided to move to Norfolk and had chosen the village of Fryfam by sticking a pin in the map. A call to the Fryfam police station had put her in touch with a local estate agent, the cottage was rented, and all Agatha had to do was sell her own cottage and leave.

But the problem lay in the people who came to view the house. Either the women were too attractive and Agatha was not going to have an attractive woman living next door to James, or they were sour and grumpy, and she did not want to inflict such people on the village.

She was due to move into her rented Norfolk cottage at the beginning of October and it was now heading to the end of September. Bright-coloured autumn leaves swirled about the Cotswold Lanes. It was an Indian summer of lazy mellow sunny days and misty nights. Never had Carsely seemed more beautiful. But Agatha was determined to get rid of her obsession for James Lacey. Fryfam was probably beautiful as well.

Agatha was just stiffening up her weakening sinews when the doorbell rang. She opened the door. Two small round people stood there. "Good morning," said the woman brightly. "We are Mr. and Mrs. Baxter-Semper. We've come to view the house."

"You should have made an appointment with the estate agent," grumped Agatha.

"Oh, but we saw the board 'For Sale' outside."

"Come in," sighed Agatha. "Take a look around. You'll find me in the kitchen if you have any questions."

She hunched over a cup of black coffee at the kitchen table and lit a cigarette. Through the window, she could see her cats, Hodge and Boswell, playing in the garden. How nice to be a cat, thought Agatha bitterly. No hopeless love, no responsibility, no bills to pay, nothing else to do but wait to be fed and roll around in the sun.

She could hear the couple moving about. Then she heard the sound of drawers being opened and closed.

She went to the foot of the stairs and shouted up, "You're supposed to be looking at the *house,* not poking among my knickers." There was a shocked silence. Then they both came downstairs. "We thought you might be leaving your furniture behind," said the woman defensively.

"No, I'm putting it into storage," said Agatha wearily. "I'm renting in Norfolk until I find somewhere to buy."

Mrs. Baxter-Semper looked past her.

"Oh, is that the garden?"

"Obviously," said Agatha, blowing smoke in her direction.

"Look, Bob. We could knock down that kitchen wall and have a nice conservatory."

Oh, God, thought Agatha, one of those nasty white wood-and-glass excrescences sticking out of the back of *my* cottage.

They stood before her as if expecting her to offer them tea or coffee.

"I'll show you out," said Agatha gruffly.

As she shut the door behind them with a bang, she could hear Mrs. Baxter-Semper saying, "What a rude woman!"

"House is perfect for us, though," remarked the husband.

Agatha picked up the phone and dialled the estate agents. "I've decided not to sell at the moment. Yes, this is Mrs. Raisin. No, *I don't want to sell.* Just take your board down."

When she replaced the receiver, she felt happier than she had done for some time. Nothing could be achieved by quitting Carsely.

"So you have decided not to go to Norfolk?" exclaimed Mrs. Bloxby, the vicar's wife, later that day. "I am so glad you aren't leaving us."

"Oh, but I am going to Norfolk. May as well get a change for a bit. But I'll be back."

The vicar's wife was a pleasant-looking woman with gray hair and mild eyes. In her ladylike clothes of flat shoes, droopy tweed skirt, silk blouse and ancient cardigan, she looked the exact opposite of Agatha Raisin, a stocky figure with excellent legs in sheer stockings and sporting a short-tailored skirt and jacket. Her glossy hair was cut in a chic bob and her bearlike eyes, unlike those of Mrs. Bloxby, looked out at the world with a defensive, wary suspicion.

Although they were close friends, they still often called each other by their second names — Mrs. Bloxby, Mrs. Raisin — as was the old-fashioned custom of the Carsely Ladies' Society to which they both belonged.

They were sitting in the vicarage garden. It was a late-autumn afternoon, mellow and golden.

"And what about James Lacey?" asked Mrs. Bloxby gently.

"Oh, I've nearly forgotten about him."

The vicar's wife looked at Agatha steadily. The day was quiet. One late rose bloomed in red glory against the mellow golden walls of the vicarage. Beyond the garden lay the churchyard, the sloping gravestones sending shadows across the tussocky grass. The clock in the church tower bonged out six o'clock.

"The nights are drawing in," said Agatha. "Well, no, I haven't got over James. That's the idea of going away. Out of sight, out of mind."

"Doesn't work." Mrs. Bloxby tugged at a loose piece of wool on her cardigan. "You're letting someone live rent-free in your head."

"That's therapy-speak," said Agatha defensively.

"None the less, it's true. You'll go to Norfolk but he'll still be there with you until you make an effort to eject him. I hope you don't get involved in any more murders, Agatha, but there are times when I wish someone would murder James."

"That's a terrible thing to say!"

"Can't help it. Never mind. Anyway, why Norfolk, why this village, what's it called again, Fryfarm?"

"I stuck a pin in a map. You see, this fortune-teller told me I should go."

"No wonder the churches are empty," said Mrs. Bloxby, half to herself. "I find that people who go to clairvoyants and fortune-tellers lack spirituality."

Agatha felt uncomfortable. "I'm only going for a giggle."

"An expensive giggle — to rent a cottage. Winter in Norfolk. It will be very cold."

"It will be very cold here."

"True, but Norfolk is so . . . flat."

"Sounds like a line from Noel Coward."

"I'll miss you," said Mrs. Bloxby. "I suppose you will want me to phone you if James comes back?"

"No . . . well, yes."

"I thought so. Let's have some tea."

Agatha found the day of her departure

arriving too soon. All her desire to flee Carsely had left her. But the weather was still sunny and unusually mild, and she had paid a hefty deposit on the cottage in Fryfam and so she reluctantly began to pack suitcases into the boot of her car, and also on the new luggage rack of the roof.

On the morning of her departure, she left her house keys with her cleaner, Doris Simpson, and then returned home to coax Hodge and Boswell into their cat boxes. She drove off down Lilac Lane, cast one longing look at James's cottage, turned the corner and then sped up the leafy hill out of Carsely, the cats in their boxes on the back seat and a road map spread beside her on the passenger seat.

The sun shone all the way until she reached the boundaries of the county of Norfolk and then the sky clouded over the brooding flat countryside.

Norfolk became part of East Anglia after the invasion of the Anglo-Saxons in the fifth century, Norfolk meaning "Home of the North Folk." The area was originally the largest swampland in England. The higher places were sites of Roman stations. The Romans attempted drainage and built a few roads across the Fens, as the marshland is called. But after the arrival of the Anglo-

Saxons, their work was left to decay, and the first effective drainage system was not developed until the seventeenth century, consisting of a series of dikes and channels.

Agatha, used to the twisting roads and hills of the Cotswolds, found all this flatness, stretching as far as the eye could see, infinitely depressing.

She pulled into a lay-by and studied the map. The cats scrabbled restlessly behind her. "Soon be there," she called to them. She could not find Fryfam. She took out an ordnance survey map of the area and at last found it. She consulted the road map again now that she knew where it was and the name seemed to leap up at her. Why hadn't she seen it a minute ago? It nestled in the middle of a network of country roads. She carefully wrote down the road numbers of all the roads leading to the village and then set off again. The sky was getting darker and a thin drizzle was beginning to mist the windscreen.

At last, with a sigh of relief, she saw a signpost with the legend "Fryfam" on it and followed its white pointing finger. There were now pine woods on either side and the countryside was becoming hilly. Round another bend, and there was a board with "Fryfam" on it, heralding that she had arrived. She stopped again and took out the estate agent's instructions. Lavender Cottage, her new temporary home, lay in Pucks Lane on the far side of the village green.

A very large village green, thought Agatha, circling round it. There was a huddle of houses with flint walls, a pub, a church, and then, running along by the graveyard, lay Pucks Lane. It was very narrow and she drove slowly along, hoping she did not meet a car coming the other way. Agatha was hopeless at reversing. She switched on her headlights. Then she saw a faded sign, "Pucks Lane," and turned left and bumped along a side lane. The cottage lay at the end of it. It was a two-storey, brick-and-flint building which seemed very old. It sagged slightly towards a large garden, a very large garden. Agatha got stiffly out and peered over the hedge at it.

The estate agent had said the key would be under the doormat. She bent down and located it. It was a large key, like the key to an old church door. It was stiff in the lock, but with a wrench, she managed to unlock the door. She found a switch on the inside of the door, put on the light and looked around. There was a little entrance hall. On the left was a dining-room and on the right, a sitting-room. There were low black beams on the ceiling. A door at the back of the hall led into a modern kitchen.

Agatha opened cupboard doors. There were plenty of dishes and pots and pans. She went back to the car and carried in a large box of groceries. She took out two tins of cat food and opened them, put the contents into two bowls, filled two other bowls with water and then returned to the car to get her cats. When she saw them quietly feeding, she began to carry all her other luggage in. She left it all in the hall. The first things she wanted were a cup of coffee and a cigarette. Agatha had given up smoking in the car ever since she had dropped a lighted cigarette down the front of her blouse one day and had nearly had an accident.

It was when she was sitting at the kitchen table with a mug of coffee in one hand and a cigarette in the other that she realized two things. The kitchen did not have a microwave. Recently Agatha had abandoned her forays into "real" cooking and had returned to the use of the microwave. Also, the cottage was very cold. She got up and began to search for a thermostat to jack up the central heating. It was only after a futile search that she realized there were no radiators. She went into the sitting-room. There was a fireplace big enough to roast an ox in. Beside the fireplace there was a basket of logs. There was also a packet of fire-lighters and a pile of old newspapers. She lit the fire. At least the logs were dry and were soon crackling away merrily. Agatha searched through the house again. There were fireplaces in every room except the kitchen. In the kitchen, in a cupboard, she found a Calor gas heater.

This is ridiculous, thought Agatha. I'll need to spend a fortune on heating this place. She went out the front door. The garden still seemed very big. It would need the services of a gardener. The lawn was thick with fallen leaves. It was Saturday. The estate agents would not be open until Monday.

After she had unpacked her groceries and put all her frozen meals away, she opened the back door. The back garden had a washing green and little else. As she looked, she blinked a little. Odd little coloured lights were dancing around at the bottom of the garden. Fireflies? Not in cold Norfolk. She walked down the garden towards the dancing lights, which abruptly disappeared on her approach.

Her stomach rumbled, reminding her it was some time since she had eaten. She decided to lock up and walk down to the pub and see if she could get a meal. She was half-way down the lane when she realized with a groan that she had not unpacked the cats' litter boxes. She returned to the cottage and attended to that chore and then set out again.

The pub was called the Green Dragon. A badly executed painting of a green dragon hung outside the door of the pub. She went in. There were only a few customers, all men, all very small men. They watched her progress to the bar in silence.

It was a silent pub, no music, no fruit machines, no television. There was no one behind the bar. Agatha's stomach gave another rumble. "Any service here?" she shouted. She turned and looked at the other customers, who promptly all looked at the stone-flagged floor.

She turned impatiently back to the bar. What sort of hell-hole have I arrived in? she thought bitterly. There was the rapid clacking of approaching high heels and then a vision appeared on the other side of the bar. She was a Junoesque blonde like a figurehead on a ship. She had thick blond — real blond — hair, which flowed back from her smooth peaches-and-cream face in soft waves. Her eyes were very wide and very blue.

"How can I help you, missus?" she asked in a soft voice.

"I'm hungry," said Agatha. "Got anything to eat?"

"I'm so sorry. We don't do meals."

"Oh, for heaven's sake," howled a much exasperated Agatha. "Is there anywhere in this village that time forgot where I can get food?"

"Reckon as how you're lucky. I got a helping of our own steak pie left. Like some?"

She gave Agatha a dazzling smile. "Yes, I would," said Agatha, mollified.

She held up a flap on the bar. "Come through. You'll be that Mrs. Raisin what's taken Lavender Cottage."

Agatha followed her into the back premises and into a large dingy kitchen with a scrubbed table in the centre.

"Please be seated, Mrs. Raisin."

"And you are?"

"I'm Mrs. Wilden. Can I offer you a glass of beer?"

"I wouldn't mind some wine if that isn't asking too much."

"No, not at all."

She disappeared and shortly after returned with a decanter of wine and a glass. Then she put a knife, fork and napkin in front of Agatha. She opened the oven door of an Aga cooker and took out a plate with a wedge of steak pie. She put it on a large plate and then opened another door in the cooker and took out a tray of roast potatoes. Another door and out came a dish of carrots, broccoli and peas. She put a huge plateful in front of Agatha, added a steaming jug of gravy, which she seemed to have conjured out of nowhere, and a basket of crusty rolls and a large pat of yellow butter. Not only was the food delicious but the wine was the best Agatha had ever tasted. She could not normally tell one wine from another, but she somehow knew this one was very special, and wished that her baronet friend, Sir Charles Fraith, could taste it and tell her what it was. She turned to ask Mrs. Wilden, but the beauty had disappeared back to the bar.

Agatha ate until she could eat no more. Feeling very mellow and slightly tipsy, she made her way back to the bar.

"All right, then?" asked Mrs. Wilden.

"It was all delicious," said Agatha. She took out her wallet. "How much do I owe you?"

A startled look of surprise came into those beautiful blue eyes.

"I told you, we don't do meals."

"But . . ."

"So you were welcome to my food and drink," said Mrs. Wilden. "Best go home and get some sleep. You must be tired."

"Thank you very much," said Agatha, putting her wallet away. "You and your husband must join me one evening for dinner."

"That do be kind of you, but he's dead and I'm always here."

"I'm sorry your husband's dead," said Agatha awkwardly as Mrs. Wilden held up the flap on the bar for her to pass through. "When you said 'our' steak pie, I thought . . ."

"I meant me and mother."

"Ah, well, you've been very kind. Perhaps I could buy a round of drinks for everyone here?" The customers had been talking quietly, but at Agatha's words there was a sudden silence.

"Not tonight. Don't do to spoil them, do it, Jimmy?"

Jimmy, a gnarled old man, muttered something and looked sadly at his empty tankard.

Agatha walked to the door. "Thanks again," she said. "Oh, by the way, there's these funny dancing lights at the bottom of the back garden. Is it some sort of insect like a firefly you've got in these parts?"

For a moment the silence in the pub was

absolute. Everybody seemed frozen, like statues. Then Mrs. Wilden picked up a glass and began to polish it. "We got nothing like that round here. Reckon your poor eyes were tired after the journey."

Agatha shrugged. "Could be." She went out into the night.

She remembered she had left the fire blazing and had not put a fire-guard in front of it. She ran the whole way back, terrified her beloved cats had been burnt to a crisp. She fumbled in her handbag for that ridiculous key. Need to oil the lock, she thought. She got the door open and hurtled into the sitting-room. The fire glowed red. Her cats lay stretched out in front of it. With a sigh of relief she bent down and patted their warm bodies. Then she went up to bed. There were two bedrooms, one with a double bed and one with a single. She chose the one with the double bed. It was covered in a huge, thick duvet. She explored the bathroom. It had an immersion heater. It would take ages to heat water for a bath. She switched it on, washed her face and cleaned her teeth and went to bed and fell into a sound and dreamless sleep.

The morning was bright and sunny. Agatha had a hot bath, dressed and had her usual breakfast of two cups of black coffee and three cigarettes. She let the cats out into the back garden and then, returning to the kitchen, picked up the estate agent's inventory of the contents. Agatha, an old hand at renting property, knew the importance of checking inventories. She wanted all her deposit back, and did not want it defrayed by mythical losses.

Agatha was half-way through it when there was a knock at the door. She opened and found herself confronted by four women.

The leader of them was a rangy middle-aged woman in a sleeveless padded jacket over a checked shirt. She was wearing corduroy trousers which bagged at the knee. "I'm Harriet Freemantle," she said. "I've brought you a cake. We all belong to the Fryfam Women's Group. Let me introduce you. This is Amy Worth." A small, faded woman in a droopy dress smiled shyly and handed Agatha a jar of chutney. "And Polly Dart." Large tweedy county woman with beetling eyebrows and an incipient moustache. "Brought you some of my scones," she boomed. "I'm Carrie Smiley." The last to come forward was youngish, about thirty-something, with dark hair, dark eyes, good figure in T-shirt and jeans. "I've brought along some of my elderberry wine."

"Come in, please," said Agatha. She led the way into the kitchen.

"They've done old Cutler's place quite nicely," said Harriet, as she and the others put their presents on the kitchen table.

"Cutler?" said Agatha, plugging in the kettle.

"An old man who lived here for ages. His daughter rents it," said Amy. "The cottage was a terrible mess when he died. He never threw anything away."

"I'm surprised the daughter didn't just sell it. Must be difficult to rent."

"Don't know about that," said Harriet. "You're the first."

"Coffee, everyone?" asked Agatha. There was a chorus of assent. "And perhaps we'll have some of Mrs. Freemantle's cake."

"Harriet. It's all first names."

"As you probably already know, I'm Agatha Raisin. I belong to a ladies' society in my home village of Carsely."

"A *ladies'* society?" exclaimed Carrie. "Is that what you call it?"

"We're a bit old-fashioned," said Agatha. "And we call each other by our second names." Harriet was efficiently cutting a delicious chocolate cake into slices and arranging the slices on plates. I'll put on pounds if

I'm not careful, thought Agatha. First that gynormous meal at the pub and now chocolate cake.

When the coffee was poured, they all took their cups and plates through to the sitting-room. "Should I light the fire?" asked Agatha.

"No, we're all warm enough," said Harriet without consulting the others.

"I think they might at least have had some sort of central heating," complained Agatha. "The rental was expensive enough without having to pay for wood."

"Oh, but you've plenty of wood," said Polly. "There's a shed at the bottom of the garden full of logs."

"I didn't see it. But it was dark when I arrived. Oh, by the way, I saw these odd lights dancing about at the bottom of the garden."

There was a silence and then Carrie asked, "Is anything missing?"

"I'm just in the middle of checking the inventory, so I don't know. Why?"

There was another silence.

Then Harriet said, "We wondered whether you would like to be an honorary member of our women's group while you're here. We're quilting."

"What's that?" mumbled Agatha, her

mouth full of cake. Why wouldn't they talk about those lights?

"We're making patchwork quilts. You know, we sew squares of coloured cloth onto old blankets."

Competitive as ever, Agatha Raisin would not admit she could not sew. "Sounds like fun," she lied. "Might drop in sometime. It is so very kind of you all to bring me all these presents."

"Tonight," said Harriet. "We meet tonight. I'll come and pick you up at seven o'clock, right after evening service. Are you C of E?"

"Yes," said Agatha, who wasn't really anything but felt that her friendship with Mrs. Bloxby qualified her for membership in the Church of England.

"Oh, in that case, I'll see you in church this evening and we'll go on from there," said Harriet.

Agatha was just about to lie and say she was feeling too poorly to go anywhere, when Polly said abruptly, "Well, go on. Tell us about your broken heart."

Agatha reddened. "What are you talking about?"

"When we heard you were coming," said Harriet, "and that you lived in a village in the Cotswolds, we wondered why you would

26

want to rent in another village and so we decided you had man trouble and wanted to get away."

I'm going off you lot rapidly, thought Agatha. She smiled round at them all, that sharklike smile which meant Agatha Raisin was about to tell a whopping lie.

"Actually I'm writing a book at the moment," she said. "I wanted somewhere to write and have peace and quiet. You see, old friends from London keep dropping down on visits and I don't have enough time for myself. I'll go along with you tonight, but I am afraid I'm going to be a bit of a recluse."

"What are you writing?" asked Amy.

"A detective story."

"What's it called?"

"*Death at the Manor*," said Agatha, improvising wildly.

"And who's your detective?"

"A baronet."

"You mean you're doing another sort of Lord Peter Wimsey?"

"Do you mind if I don't talk about my work anymore?" said Agatha. "I don't like discussing it."

"Just tell us," said Amy, leaning forward. "Have you had any published?"

"No, this is my first attempt. I am a real-life detective, so I thought I may as well fictionalize some of my adventures."

"You mean you work for the police?" asked Harriet.

"I occasionally work *with* the police," said Agatha grandly. She proceeded to brag about her cases. To her irritation, just as she had got to the exciting bit of one of them, Harriet rose and said abruptly, "Sorry, we've got to go."

Agatha saw them out. She walked with them down to the garden gate and waved them goodbye. She stayed leaning on the gate, enjoying the sunshine.

Harriet's voice travelled back to her ears. "Of course she was lying."

"Do you think so?" Amy's voice.

"Oh, yes. Not a word of truth in any of it. Woman probably can't write a word."

Agatha clenched her fists. Jealous cow. She would show her. She *would* write a book. Writing was writing and she had written enough press releases in her days as a public relations officer. She had brought her computer and printer with her. She began to feel quite excited. When her name topped the best-seller list, then James would sit up and take notice.

On her road back to the house, she peered over the hedge at the driveway at the side of the house where her car was parked. What had they meant by asking if anything was missing?

She opened the kitchen door and went down to the bottom of the garden, finding a shed behind a stand of trees. It was full of logs. She returned to the kitchen with the cats scampering at her heels. At least they're happy with the place, she thought. She fed them and returned to checking the inventory, but all the while wondering about her visitors. Did they have husbands? They couldn't all be widows.

After she had finished ticking off everything on the inventory, she scraped out the contents of Genuine Bengali Curry into a pot. She would need to buy a microwave. She ate the hot mess and then decided to get down to writing that book.

She set up the computer on the kitchen table, typed in "Chapter One," and then stared at the screen. She found that instead of writing that book, she was beginning to write down excuses to get out of quilting. "I suffer from migraine." No good. They'd all call around with pills. "Something urgent has come up." What? And how on earth could she get in touch with them? Mrs. Wilden at the pub would know.

She decided to walk down to the pub.

Agatha, as she trudged down Pucks Lane,

decided she had better start observing everything about the countryside. Writers did that. The red berries of hips and haws could be seen in the hedgerow to her right. Okay. "The red berries of hips and haws shone like jewelled lamps . . ." No, scrub that. "The scarlet berries of hips and haws hung like lamps over the . . ."

Nope, try again. "Hawthorn berries starred the hedgerow." No, berries can't star. Flowers can. Who the hell wants to be a writer anyway?

The pub was closed. Agatha stood irresolute. In the middle of the village green was a duck pond, minus ducks. There was a bench overlooking it. She crossed over and sat down and stared at the water.

"Afternoon."

Agatha jumped nervously. A gnarled old man had sat quietly down beside her.

"Afternoon," said Agatha.

He shuffled along the bench until he was sitting close to her. He smelt of ham soup and cigarette smoke. He was obviously in his Sunday best, to judge from the old hairy suit, the white shirt and striped tie. His large boots were highly polished.

Then Agatha felt something on her knee, and looking down, saw that he had placed one old hand on it.

Agatha lifted up his hand and placed it on his own knee. "Behave yourself," she said sharply.

"Don't you go worriting about that fellow back home who done you wrong. Us'll look after you."

Agatha rose and strode off, her face flaming. Had the whole village decided she had a broken heart? Damn them all. She would see the estate agent first thing on Monday morning and say she wanted to cancel.

She found a street leading off the far end of the village green which had a small selection of shops. There were a post office-cum-general store like the one in Carsely, an electrical-goods shop, one selling Laura Ashley–type clothes, an antique shop, and at the end, Bryman's, the estate agent. She studied the cards in the window. House prices were less than in the Cotswolds, but not much less.

She wandered back to the village green, as lonely as a cloud, and decided to go back home and spend a useful day unpacking the rest of her stuff.

The gardener called during the afternoon and asked her if there was anything in particular she would like to have done. Agatha said she would like him to sweep the leaves, mow the lawn and keep the flower-beds tidy.

31

He was a young man, muscled and tattooed, with a thick thatch of nut-brown hair. He said his name was Barry Jones and he would call round on the next day. Agatha thanked him and as he turned to go, she said, "Do you know anything about odd lights? I saw odd little lights dancing around at the bottom of the garden last night."

He did not even turn around. "Reckon I don't know nothing about that," he said and walked away with a rapid pace.

There's something odd about those lights, thought Agatha. Maybe it's some wretched poisonous insect and the locals don't want to put off visitors to the village by telling them about it.

She went back to her housekeeping duties, wondering as she hung away clothes whether the log fires would be enough to keep the house warm in a cold spell. The estate agent should have warned her.

When she realized it was nearly six o'clock, she began to wonder whether she should get out of going to church and then quilting. She checked the TV Guide she had brought with her. There was nothing much on. And, she realized, she was lonely.

She locked up and walked round to the church in time for evensong. To her amazement, in these godless days, the church was full. The vicar's sermon dealt with faith as opposed to superstition, and Agatha's mind drifted back to those lights. There was a closed, inbred anachronistic feel to this village. All across the world raged fire and floods and famine. Yet here in Fryfam, hatted ladies and suited gents raised their voices in "Abide With Me" as if nothing existed outside their safe English world governed by the changing seasons and the church calendar: Michaelmas, Candlemas, Harvest Festival, Advent, Christmas.

She waited in the churchyard. Harriet approached her surrounded by the three others she had met earlier. They were wearing the same clothes but had put on hats — Harriet a felt pudding basin, Amy a straw, Polly Dart a tweed fishing hat and Carrie sporting a baseball cap.

Agatha, who had changed into a tailored trouser suit and silk blouse, felt almost over-dressed.

"Right," said Harriet. "Off we go!"

A couple passed their group, arguing acrimoniously. "Don't be such a *bore*, Tolly," said the woman. A waft of Gucci's Envy reached Agatha's nostrils. She paused, looking after the couple. The woman had what Agatha thought of as the "new" beauty, meaning others admired it. She had blond hair worn down to her shoulders. She was wearing a well-tailored tweed suit, the skirt of which had a slit up one side, revealing a well-shaped leg clothed in a ten-denier stocking — stockings, not tights, for the slit was long enough to show a flash of stocking top. Her eyes were pale blue and well set apart. She had high cheek-bones, but her nose was set too close to her mouth and her long mouth too close to her square chin. He was older, small, plump and choleric, with thinning hair and a high colour.

"Come on, Agatha," ordered Harriet.

"Who are they? That couple?"

"Oh, that's our squire, self-appointed, made his money out of bathroom showers, and his wife, Lucy. The Trumpington-Jameses. Funny, isn't it," said Harriet, her voice carrying across the churchyard. "Not so long ago a double-barrelled name de- noted a lady or gentleman. Now it means it's some lower-middle-class parvenu."

"Aren't you being a bit snobby?" asked Agatha.

"No," said Harriet. "They're quite awful, as you'll find out."

"How will I find out?"

"They'll think it their squire-archical duty to welcome the newcomer. You'll see."

"Where are we going?"

"My place."

Harriet's place was on the far side of the green, a square, early Victorian house.

Leading the way into a large, if gloomy, sitting-room, Harriet switched on the lamps and said, "Anyone for a drink first?" And before a grateful Agatha could ask for a gin and tonic, Harriet said, "I know, we'll have some of Carrie's elderberry wine."

Agatha looked about her. The room had long windows and a high ceiling but was crowded with heavy pieces of furniture. The walls were painted a dull green and hung with dingy paintings of horses and dead game.

Amy was getting blankets and boxes of cloth and sewing implements out of a large chest in the corner.

"I think you should share a quilt with Carrie," said Amy. "You work on the one end and she'll work on the other. If you sit side by side, you can spread the blanket out between you."

Harriet returned with a tray of glasses full of elderberry wine. Agatha sipped hers cautiously. It was very sweet and tasted slightly medicinal.

"Are we all widows here?" asked Agatha, looking around. "No husbands?"

"My husband's in the pub with Amy's and

Polly's," said Harriet. "Carrie's divorced."

"I thought the pub was closed on Sundays. I went round at lunch-time and it was closed."

"Opens Sunday evenings." Harriet drained her glass and put it back on the tray. "We'd best get started."

It should be simple, thought Agatha, as Carrie handed her a little pile of squares of cloth. Just stitch them on.

"Not like that," said Carrie, as Agatha stabbed a needle into the edge of one. "You hem it first and then stitch it on and unpick the hem." Agatha scowled horribly and proceeded to try to hem a slippery little square of silk. Just as soon as it got a stitch in it, the silk frayed at the edges. She surreptitiously dropped it on the floor and picked out a piece of coloured wool. She glanced sideways at Carrie, who was placing neat little, almost invisible, stitches, rapidly in squares of material.

She decided to start up a conversation to try to distract the others from her amateur sewing. "Mrs. Wilden at the pub treated me to an excellent meal last night. She's quite stunningly beautiful."

"Pity she's got the morals of a tom-cat," snapped Polly, biting a thread with strong yellow teeth.

"Oh, really?" said Agatha, looking around curiously at the set faces. "I found her rather sweet."

"Good thing you're not married." Amy, sounding almost tearful.

"When did your husband die, Agatha?" asked Carrie.

"A while back," said Agatha. "I don't want to talk about it." She did not want to tell them her husband had been murdered right after he had surfaced from the past to stop her marrying James Lacey. "I'm still wondering about those lights," she went on. She noticed with surprise that because of the distraction of talking she had actually managed to hem a square of cloth.

"Have you seen them again?" asked Harriet.

"No."

"Well, there you are. You were probably tired after the long drive and thought you saw them."

Agatha gave up on the subject of the lights. She was sure these women probably gossiped easily among themselves. She was the outsider, not yet accepted, and that was putting the brakes on any conversation.

She felt she was being let out of school when Harriet said after an hour, "Well, that's it for tonight."

As Agatha was leaving, she stopped to admire an arrangement of autumn leaves in a vase in the hall. Harriet lifted out the bunch of leaves and thrust it at Agatha. "Take it," she said. "I dip the leaves in glycerine so they should last you the winter."

Agatha walked homewards bearing the leaves. She remembered there was a large stone jar on the floor by the fireplace in the sitting-room. She let herself into the cottage, glad that she had brought her cats for company as Hodge and Boswell undulated about her ankles.

She walked through to the kitchen and put the bunch of leaves on the kitchen counter. She looked out the window and the dancing lights were there again.

Agatha unlocked the door and walked down the garden. The lights had disappeared.

Muttering to herself, she walked back to the house. Something funny was going on. She had not imagined those lights and there was nothing wrong with her eyesight.

She walked through to the sitting-room to get that vase. It was no longer there. Agatha began to wonder if she had imagined it. She took the inventory out of the kitchen drawer. Yes, there it was under "Contents of Sitting-Room" — one pottery vase.

Agatha suddenly felt threatened. She checked the doors were locked and went up to bed. Her stomach rumbled, reminding her she had not had any dinner, but the thought of going downstairs again frightened her. She bathed and undressed and crawled under the duvet and pulled it over her head to shut out the terrors of the night.

TWO

†

Another sunny morning and Agatha, ashamed of her night-time fears, decided to drive into Norwich, buy a microwave, have breakfast, and then return to tackle the estate agent over the lack of central heating.

Being in Norwich brightened up the feelings of city-bred Agatha immensely. She bought a microwave and a further supply of microwavable meals in Marks & Spencer, had a large cholesterol-filled breakfast, bought a cheap glass vase, and returned to Fryfam in a confident frame of mind.

After she had unpacked her shopping and fed her cats, she walked to the estate agent's.

She pushed open the door of Bryman's and walked in. To her intense irritation, she saw the droopy figure of Amy Worth sitting behind a computer screen. "Why didn't you tell me you worked here?" complained Agatha.

"There didn't seem much point," said

Amy defensively. "I'm just the typist. I don't have anything to do with the renting of the houses."

"So who do I speak to?"

"Mr. Bryman. I'll get him."

Secretive about nothing at all, fumed Agatha. Amy re-emerged and held open the door to an inner office. "Mr. Bryman will see you now."

Agatha walked past her. A youngish man with a sallow face, thick lips and wet eyes stood up and extended his hand. "Welcome, Mrs. Raisin."

Agatha shook his hand, which was clammy. What a damp young man, she thought. He was in shirt-sleeves and there were patches of sweat under his armpits. There was also an unpleasant goaty smell emanating from him. Amy, Agatha had noticed, was wearing the same clothes she had worn the day before. Perhaps no one in Fryfam bothered about baths.

Agatha sat down. "You should have warned me there was no central heating," she began.

"But the logs are free," he protested. "Stacks of logs."

"I do not want to have to set and clean all those fireplaces when the weather turns cold."

"We'll let you have a couple of Calor gas heaters like the one in the kitchen. I'll bring them round today."

"Don't you have anywhere else?"

"Not to rent. For sale only. Quite a lot of the houses in Fryfam are second homes. People leave them empty in the winter. Only come down for the summer months. There's always a demand for second homes. You'll find there's few of us here in the winter."

"Okay, I'll take the heaters. Now, there's something else."

He raised his eyebrows in query.

"I checked the inventory yesterday. There was definitely a stone vase in the sitting-room. Well, it's disappeared. I saw these lights at the end of the garden and went to investigate and when I came back the vase had gone."

"Oh, I think we can overlook that, Mrs. Raisin. It's just an old vase."

"I am not going to overlook it," said Agatha stubbornly. "Is there a policeman here? There must be. I phoned the police to get your name."

"There's PC Framp, but I wouldn't bother — "

"I will bother. Where is he? I didn't see a police station."

"It's out a bit on the road to the manor house."

"Which is where?"

"North of the village green. The road that goes out of the village the opposite way to the one you arrived on."

"Right. When will you be arriving with the heaters?"

"I've got a spare key. I'll leave them in the hall if you aren't in."

"Don't upset my cats."

"I didn't know you had pets, Mrs. Raisin. You didn't say anything about cats."

Agatha rose to her feet and looked at him truculently. "And you didn't say anything about not having them. No cats, no rental."

She turned and marched out. She ignored Amy. She was fed up with the whole bunch of them. And she had only just arrived!

She decided to drive. She returned home to get in her car and saw a square envelope lying inside the door. She opened it up. There was a note on stiff parchment. "We would like to welcome you to the village. Please come for tea this afternoon at four o'clock. Lucy Trumpington-James."

Summoned to the manor house, thought Agatha. Well, God knows, I've got nothing better to do.

She phoned Mrs. Bloxby in Carsely. "Haven't heard from James," said the vicar's wife promptly. "I wasn't phoning about that," lied Agatha. "Just wondered how everyone was getting on."

"Same as ever." said Mrs. Bloxby cheerfully. "What's that place in Norfolk like?"

"Weird," said Agatha. "It's a small village and I gather a large proportion of the population only use their houses in summer, which is enough to turn anyone Communist when you think of the housing shortage."

"Well, your house is going to be empty for the winter. Would you like me to find a homeless family?"

"No, don't," said Agatha, repressing a shudder.

"I thought not." Was the saintly Mrs. Bloxby being *catty?* Perish the thought.

"It's about these strange lights." Agatha told her all about them and about the locals' reluctance to even discuss them.

"You've a mystery to solve," said Mrs. Bloxby.

"I'm supposed to be meeting my destiny here, according to that fortune-teller."

"It's early days. You've only just arrived. I'm sure you'll stir something up. Oh, Charles phoned. Wanted to know where you were."

Agatha thought briefly of Sir Charles Fraith, lightweight, tightwad, fickle. "No, if my destiny is to meet some fellow, I don't want him hanging around."

"So, any eligible men around?"

"Apart from some gnarled old codger who put his hand on my knee and a sweaty estate agent, I haven't met any. And this cottage has no central heating, nothing but log fires."

"The weather can get grim over there. Are you sure you don't want to come back? You could use the lack of central heating as an excuse."

"Not yet, but you're right. I can leave this place any time I want. I meant to tell that estate agent I was leaving, but I'll hang on a bit longer."

After she had rung off, Agatha felt much cheered. Of course, she could simply pack up and go. But first, see what the local copper had to say.

She drove out of the village a little way and soon saw the police station. She parked outside and went and rang the bell. There was a police car on the short drive at the side, so she was sure PC Framp was at home.

After some minutes, the door was opened. PC Framp was a tall, thin man with receding hair above a lugubrious face. He had an apron on and was holding a frying pan.

"It's my day off," he said defensively.

Agatha ignored that. "My name is Agatha Raisin and I have just rented Lavender Cottage. There have been peculiar lights at the bottom of my garden and a vase is missing."

"Come in," he said wearily. "But don't mind if I cook my lunch."

Agatha followed him through the police office, and then along a corridor to a stone-flagged kitchen. It was amazingly dirty and smelt of sour milk. It was also very hot. The policeman put the frying pan on top of an Aga cooker, poured in oil, cracked in two eggs, then added two rashers of bacon and two slices of bread. A fine mist of fat rose from the pan and covered the already greasy black top of the cooker.

She sat down at a crumby plastic-topped kitchen table. She leaned her elbows on it and then realized she had put one elbow in a smear of marmalade. At last Framp shoveled the mess out of the frying pan onto a chipped and cracked plate and sat down opposite her.

"So," began Agatha impatiently, "what about these lights?"

"Some kids playing pranks."

"So you know that for a fact?"

"Educated guess." He stabbed the corner of a piece of fried bread into the yolk of an egg and shoved it in his mouth.

"So you don't *really* know?"

He chomped steadily, filled a mug with tea, took a great swallow, wiped his mouth with the back of his hand and then said, "Nothing important's ever taken. Just bits and pieces. A worthless picture, a cream jug, three forks, things like that."

"Why don't you come round to my cottage and fingerprint the place?"

"I don't fingerprint things. CID does that and they ain't going to come running over with their kit and the forensic boys over a load of junk."

"It doesn't seem to bother you that someone is frightening the village with their antics. They won't talk about it."

"Well, no, they wouldn't. Not to you."

"Why?"

"They think it's fairies."

Agatha stared at him and then said, "Oh, come on. Fairies at the bottom of the garden!"

"Fact."

"Fairies are not fact! And you've got egg on your chin. Look, the women I've met are not inbred peasants. They wouldn't believe in fairies."

"That they do. Some have been putting salt round their houses to keep the fairies away, others are leaving gifts like saucers of milk and things like that."

Agatha looked at him, puzzled, and then her face cleared. "Oh, I know what it is. You're pulling my leg."

"No. I'm telling you, Mrs. Raisin. This is a very old part of Britain and strange things do happen here."

"I don't believe in fairies and I don't think you do either." Agatha got to her feet. "I won't waste any more of your time. I'll solve the mystery myself. I am by way of being a detective."

She turned at the kitchen door and looked back, but he was dunking the last of his fried bread in the remaining egg.

Agatha got in her car in a bad temper. She drove slowly along until she came to a lodge-gate. This then must be the manor. She checked her watch. Three-thirty. Too early. She lowered the windows. The village of Fryfam nestled in pine woods and the air was sweet with the scent. A lazy bee blundered into the car, as if bewildered by all this late sunshine and warmth. Agatha wondered whether to swat it, but then realized she could not. She shrank back in her seat until it blundered out again.

Fairies, indeed! She decided furiously that the lazy policeman was probably trying to take the mickey out of a tourist.

Her thoughts turned to the vicar's wife, Mrs. Bloxby. Agatha knew that Mrs. Bloxby did not approve of her ongoing love for James Lacey and felt irritated. She should be sympathetic, understanding and supportive. Still, surely the whole reason for her flight to Norfolk, apart from the fortune-teller's prophecy, was to get James out of her hair. Not for a moment would she admit to herself that the real reason was because she wanted him to return to Carsely, find her gone and miss her.

She tried to jerk her thoughts back to the mystery of the dancing lights, but they kept returning to the way she would behave when she saw him again and what she would say. So immersed was she in her thoughts that it was with a start of surprise she realized the clock on the dashboard was registering five minutes past four. She started the car and turned into the drive. The pine trees were thick on either side. She was just wondering if she would ever reach the house when she turned a bend in the drive, and there it was, a square eighteenth-century building like a hunting-box, with a Victorian servants' wing stuck on one side. It had a small porticoed entrance with a very new coat of arms stuck on top. Two heraldic beasts supported a shield. Agatha squinted up as she got out of the car but could not make out the details. What had the Trumpington-Jameses put on their shield? Bathroom showers rampant?

She rang the bell at the side of the door. Lucy Trumpington-James answered the door wearing a gold silk Armani suit and a quantity of gold jewellery, chains round the neck and bracelets on her thin wrists.

"Come in," she said. "Tolly's in the drawing-room."

Agatha followed her across a dark hall with console tables topped with Chinese vases of autumn leaves. Harriet's work?

The drawing-room came as a shock to Agatha, who had been expecting something country-house with chintz, Persian rugs, and oil paintings. There were two large oatmeal sofas in front of the fire, the sort you made up of blocks of chairs. In front of them was an oblong black-lacquered table. The walls were painted blood-red and the fitted carpet was a gleaming expanse of white. The paintings were modern abstracts. The side tables were of white lacquer and covered with photo frames holding pictures of the

Trumpington-Jameses out hunting, at parties, at Henley, at Ascot and various other fashionable places. A black-lacquered wall unit held a television set, a CD player and very new and unread-looking books. The fire was one of those electric fake-log ones. The room was bright, lit by a crystal chandelier overhead, and by angular brass standard lamps in corners.

"Do sit down, Mrs. Raisin," said Tolly Trumpington-James, rising to meet her. He was wearing a hacking jacket and cavalry-twill trousers. His Tattersall shirt was open at the neck.

"Call me Agatha," said Agatha, sitting down. She scanned the room for signs of an ashtray but could see none. She gave a little sigh, but at least it would keep her off fags for an hour.

Lucy rang a bell in the wall beside the fireplace. Its summons was answered, not by a neat maid, but by a fat, surly-looking woman in a stained gingham pinafore.

"We'll have tea now, Betty," said Lucy.

"And then I'm off," said surly Betty. "You'll need to clear up yourselves." She clumped off in a pair of battered boots.

"Help these days," said Lucy, raising her eyes. "Do you have trouble with help, Agatha?"

Not so long ago, the old Agatha, intimidated at being in a manor house, would have invented colourful stories about a whole regiment of servants. Now she simply said, "I don't have any trouble back home. I have an excellent cleaning woman who comes in twice a week."

"Lucky you," sighed Lucy. "I sometimes wish we had never come here."

"Why did you?" asked Agatha curiously.

"Made my pile," said Tolly. "Wanted a bit of country life. Get a bit of hunting."

"And because he wants to act the squire, we're stuck here," said Lucy with a light laugh.

Her husband flashed her an angry look, but the door opened and Betty lumbered in with a large tray which she deposited on the low table in front of them. Besides tea, there was a plate with a few chocolate biscuits — no sandwiches, no fruit-cake.

"That will be all, Betty," said Tolly imperiously.

"Should think so, too," grumbled Betty and off she went.

"Such a character," murmured Lucy, clanking her bangles.

People who would not pay good wages and put up with surly help were usually tight with money, thought Agatha.

"We had such a nice place in London. Kensington," said Lucy, pouring tea. "Help yourself to milk and sugar, Agatha. Do you know Kensington?"

"Yes, very well. I used to live in London. I had a public relations business. I took early retirement to move to the Cotswolds."

"Don't you miss London?"

"I did when I first moved to the country, but then a lot of exciting and scary things happened, and Carsely — that's where I live — began to seem more interesting than London."

There was a slight snore. Tolly had fallen asleep, his teacup resting on his paunch.

Lucy sighed, rose and took the cup from him.

"If only we could get back to London," she mourned. "But he wants to be the country gentleman. Doesn't work. None of the county invite us unless they want money for some charity or other. I tried to get that coat of arms taken down."

"Doesn't it come from the College of Arms or something?"

"No, he had an artist make it up for him. He got some poncey interior designer to do this room. Isn't it foul?"

"It's a bit . . . modern."

"It's vulgar."

"Could you rent in London for the winter?"

"He won't think of it. He likes to keep me trapped here. So tell me, what on earth could be exciting about living in the Cotswolds?"

Agatha chattered on happily about her amazing detective abilities until she realized she was boring Lucy, so she finished by saying, "You have an interesting mystery here in Fryfam."

"Like what?" Lucy stifled a yawn.

"The fairies. The dancing lights."

"Oh, those. I'm telling you, once the second-home people go back to London, you're left with a lot of inbred peasants who'd believe anything."

"But I met the women's group members. They seem intelligent."

"Yes, but they're all from Fryfam, don't you see? You've never spent a winter here, have you?"

Agatha shook her head.

"It's so black and bleak and grim, you'll end up believing in fairies yourself."

Lucy yawned again.

Agatha rose to her feet. "I must go."

"Must you? Can you find your own way out?"

"Sure. Perhaps you would like to have tea with me?"

"Too kind. I'll let you know."

Agatha hesitated in the hall, looking in her handbag for her car keys. "Wake up, Tolly," she heard Lucy say sharply. "She's gone."

"Thank God for that. Another plain woman and not quite one of us."

"Not quite one of *who?*" demanded Lucy shrilly. "It's because of your snobbery that we're stuck in this dump."

Agatha walked quickly away, her face flaming. She had moved a long way away from the Birmingham slum of her upbringing, but at weak moments she thought that people could still sniff it out.

She got in the car and drove home and phoned Mrs. Bloxby. "You can give Charles my number and address and tell him if he's at loose ends, I've got a spare room."

"I'll tell him. How are those mysterious lights?"

"The locals believe they are fairies."

"How interesting! You're in the Breckland area of Norfolk, aren't you?"

"Am I?"

"Yes, I looked it up on the map. Very old part. There are tumuli and old flint quarries called Grimes Graves. Old places often make people superstitious. I think it's something in the soil."

"Well, I don't believe in fairies. Probably kids."

"Children? Got a lot of them in the village?"

"Come to think of it, I haven't seen one."

"Good hunting. Alf's just come home."

Alf was the vicar, who did not approve of Agatha Raisin.

"Right, talk to you soon." Agatha said goodbye and rang off. Then she felt petty. She had only wanted Charles to come to throw a baronet in Tolly's vulgar face.

Then she noticed two Calor gas heaters tucked at the side of the hall. She was beginning to think that all these tales of a grim winter were probably exaggerations and hoped she hadn't made a fuss about nothing.

She took a look in the back garden. Barry was mowing the lawn. It was a bit too late to put through a load of washing and hang it out. She wondered what the weather forecast was. She had not switched on the television set or the radio since her arrival.

Barry waved through the window to her and left. Agatha decided to try that book again. She wrote the title, "Death at the Manor." She had been to the manor, so that was a start. She would start by describing

Lucy and Tolly and their vulgar drawing-room and go on from there.

To her surprise, she had managed to write four pages before the doorbell rang. Amy stood on the doorstep. "I came to say how sorry I am that I didn't tell you I worked for the estate agents. But you see, if anything was wrong, I thought you would blame me."

"Come in," Agatha said reluctantly. She saved what she had written and switched off the computer.

"Oh, I've interrupted your writing," said Amy. "You must be furious with me."

"Not at all. Come through to the kitchen." Agatha squinted at her watch. Six-thirty in the evening. "Do you want some dinner? I haven't eaten."

"If you're sure . . ."

"No, it's frozen Marks's stuff. Sit down. Don't you have dinner with your husband?"

"Jerry's in the pub." Amy's eyes filled with tears.

"Oh, dear. The beautiful Mrs. Wilden?"

"Yes." Amy took out a small square of handkerchief and blew her nose fiercely. "She's taken away all our husbands. Harriet wants her tarred and feathered."

Agatha fished out a bottle of Gordon's gin she had brought with her. "Drink?"

"Please."

Agatha made two large gin and tonics. Then she took out two frozen packets of lasagna and put the first one in the microwave, and when that was done, put in the second, then gave the first an extra twirl.

She served the meals and then, sitting down opposite Amy, asked, "What does your husband do?"

"He works for a seed company just outside Norwich."

"And is he having an affair with Mrs. Wilden?"

"Oh, no."

"Then what's the problem?"

"It's just that he goes to the pub every night, and so does Henry Freemantle and Peter Dart."

"Harriet's and Polly's husbands, too?"

"Yes." Amy gave a dismal sniff and poked at her lasagna.

"And all they do is go to look at the fair Mrs. Wilden?"

Amy nodded.

"And does she encourage them?"

"I don't think Rosie Wilden has to do anything special. She just is."

"So why don't you and Harriet and Polly go to the pub?"

"We couldn't do that!"

"Why?" asked Agatha patiently.

58

"It's an old-fashioned village. They don't mind women in the pub at lunchtime, but they're frowned on in the evening."

"I've never heard anything more ridiculous. I'll phone Polly and Harriet. We'll all go."

"The husbands will be furious."

"Time they were."

Agatha went through to the phone, which was in a small table in the hall. She called through to Amy, "What are their phone numbers?"

Amy gave the numbers but then started to protest. Agatha ignored her. She phoned Harriet first and said curtly that Amy was crying her eyes out, so she was taking her to the pub, and did Harriet want to come and bring Polly.

There was a silence and then Harriet said harshly, "Do you know what you are doing?"

"Well, yes. I don't see why you should all be stuck at home while your husbands are in the pub. Into battle, Harriet."

"All right," said Harriet. "I'll do it. Damn it. I'll *do* it."

"See you both there in half an hour." Agatha rang off and returned to the kitchen.

"Right, Amy," she said. "Upstairs with me. I'm going to make your face up."

"But I never wear make-up. Jerry doesn't

59

like me wearing make-up."

"I think your trouble is you always do what Jerry wants. Upstairs."

Agatha deftly worked on Polly's face — foundation cream, powder, blusher, mascara, eye-shadow and lipstick. "There!" she said a last. "You look more like a human being."

She jerked open her wardrobe door and took out a black dress. "Pop this on. What size of shoes do you wear?"

"Fives. But — "

"You need heels. Nothing like heels to give you confidence. Get a move on."

Amy, used to bending to any will stronger than her own, meekly put on the little black dress and a pair of high-heeled shoes. Agatha put some gold jewellery round her neck. "Now, straighten your shoulders. Right. Great. Forward march!"

Harriet and Polly were waiting outside the pub. "You look glamorous, Amy," said Harriet. This was a wild exaggeration, but had the effect of making Amy smile with delight.

"Here we go," said Agatha Raisin and pushed open the door.

Behind the bar, in the low, smoky room full of men, Rosie Wilden glowed like a jewel. She was wearing a soft white chiffon blouse with a plunging neckline.

Agatha found a table in a corner for her new friends. Silence had fallen at their entrance and the silence continued as Agatha walked to the bar and said to Rosie Wilden, "Have you any champagne?"

"I do indeed, Mrs. Raisin."

"Two bottles," ordered Agatha. "That's for starters."

"Big occasion?"

"Yes, my birthday," lied Agatha.

She returned through the still silent men to the table. "Our husbands are glaring at us," whispered Amy. "That's the three of them, over at the bar."

"Good," said Agatha. "Now when the champagne arrives, I want you all to sing 'Happy Birthday to You.'"

"Is it your birthday?" asked Polly.

"No, but they don't know that and you don't want to look as if you've come in to check on them."

Rosie Wilden came round the bar with a tray of glasses. Then she turned and shouted, "Barry, could you be a love and bring the bottles and ice bucket over here?"

Agatha's gardener came up with the bottles and ice bucket. He was not overwhelmingly handsome, but, decided Agatha, he was the best-looking man in the pub.

"Barry," cried Agatha. "Do join us. It's my birthday."

Barry grinned and shuffled his feet. "I'm with me two mates."

"Bring them over. We'd better have two more bottles, Mrs. Wilder."

Barry returned with his two friends and they crammed in round the table. Rosie deftly opened the first bottle. To Agatha's delight, Barry, unprompted, began to sing "Happy Birthday to You" in a strong baritone. He was joined by his friends, and then Harriet, Polly and Amy joined in.

"You have a lovely voice, Barry," said Agatha. "Know anything else?"

Barry, who had been already well oiled before he started on the champagne, got to his feet and proceeded to give them an Elvis Presley impersonation, "Jailhouse Rock," complete with gyrating hips and pretend guitar.

The three women, aware of their glaring husbands over by the bar, laughed and cheered. One of Barry's friends, Mark, a weedy youth with a rolled-up cigarette hanging from the corner of his mouth, said, "Don't half cheer the place up, a bit of a song. What about one of you ladies?"

To Agatha's amusement, Polly, slightly red about the nose — must have had a few to bolster her, thought Agatha — rose to her feet and belted out "The Fishermen of England," while they all drank steadily and more champagne appeared. The locals, hungry for a free drink, began to crowd round the table until the errant husbands were left isolated at the bar.

"Why don't those three join the party," shouted Agatha.

"That's our husbands," said Harriet.

"Your *husbands!*" Agatha affected amazement. "What on earth are they doing on their own? Do they come to ogle the barmaid?"

The three promptly came over but could not get near the table for the crowd. Agatha called for more songs and more champagne and kept the party going until Rosie called, "Time, gentlemen, please."

They all crowded out into the night. "What a marvellous evening," said Agatha loudly. "See you here tomorrow night, girls?"

The "girls" were now flanked by their glaring husbands, but Harriet said gamely, "Same time, same place, Agatha."

Agatha saw the lank figure of the village policeman crossing the green and decided to leave her car where it was. She walked home, somewhat unsteadily, let herself in and swallowed as much cold water as she could to try to stave off next morning's hangover.

Next morning, she was awakened by a furious ringing of her doorbell. She put on a dressing-gown and struggled downstairs. The clock in the hall said eight o'clock.

She opened the door, blinking in the strong sunlight, and focused on the wrathful face of Henry Freemantle.

"We want you to leave our wives alone," he said truculently.

"What on earth are you talking about?"

"That pub is for men."

"Apart from the delicious Rosie?"

He reddened. "I'm warning you."

"See this door?" said Agatha. "Take a good, close look at it."

She slammed it in his face.

What time-warp have I landed in, she thought angrily, but she felt hung over and shaken. Once more she toyed with the idea of packing up and going home. She fed the cats and let them out into the garden and went back to bed and immediately fell asleep, not waking until noon.

She showered and dressed, feeling much better. A good walk was what she needed. This glorious weather would not last forever.

She walked out on the road leading past the police station and the manor lodge. The air was sweet with the scent of pine. A hill wound upwards. She reached the top and paused in amazement. The road before her dipped down to flatland as far as the eye could see. An enormous sky stretched out over her head. She walked down and along the straight ribbon of road. She walked until she came to a broad lake bordered by reeds. A light breeze ruffled its glassy surface, which mirrored the small puffy clouds in the blue sky above. She sat down on a rock. Behind her, a stone plover called. Agatha did not know the name of the bird, only that the sound made her feel lonely and isolated.

But then the bird fell silent and after a time the loneliness ebbed, leaving her enfolded in a strange feeling of peace. She lit a cigarette and then promptly stubbed it out. Cigarettes tasted foul in fresh air. The old Agatha would have chucked the unsmoked cigarette into the lake. The new Agatha put it in her pocket, not wanting any passing duck to gobble it up.

A skein of geese flew far overhead. Agatha sat dreaming about not much in particular, soothed by the lapping of the water and the breeze rustling through the tall reeds.

At last she rose and stood up. She felt

slightly stiff and all her ease left her. She was suddenly sharply aware of being middle-aged. Was it worth all the effort to keep age at bay with exercise and anti-wrinkle creams? There was always the temptation to let it all go, let the hair grow in grey, let the chin sag and come to terms with age.

She looked towards the horizon, shading her eyes. There was a black line of cloud and thin wisps of cloud were streaming out from it like the fingers of approaching winter. The air had become cold. Diminished now by the grandeur of the spacious landscape, Agatha headed homewards, glad as she walked back up the hill again and found herself enclosed on either side by the whispering pine trees, the bleak immensity of the flatland behind her now blotted out. Her stomach rumbled, reminding herself that she had not eaten anything.

She was walking up to her cottage when she came across Lucy Trumpington-James. "I've been looking for you," she said abruptly. "What's all this about your birthday party in the pub? You might have told me."

"Come in," said Agatha, leading the way up the garden path and remembering at the same time that her car was still parked outside the pub. She unlocked the door. "I'll let you into a secret, Lucy. It wasn't really my birthday. I was just trying to cheer up the local ladies. Their husbands had deserted them to gawk at the charms of Rosie Wilden."

Lucy followed her into the kitchen and sat down at the kitchen table. "That trollop."

"Are you sure she's a trollop? She seems kind. She can't help it if she's pretty."

"Oh, yeah? Well, I think she's having an affair with Tolly."

"Have you asked him?"

"Yes, but he denies it, of course."

"So what proof do you have?"

"Rosie makes her own rose perfume. Sickly stuff. I came back from the hairdresser in Norwich and the smell of the stuff was in our bedroom, and Tolly had changed the bed and washed the sheets. When did Tolly ever wash sheets? He said some woman from the hunt committee had been round and had used our bathroom, which is off our bedroom, to repair her make-up. He pointed out that Rosie gives the perfume all round the village."

"And the sheets?"

"He says this woman took a drink up with her and spilt some on the bed."

"Oh, dear."

"I asked for her name and he went into a

fury and said I was always picking on him and he wants a divorce."

Agatha plugged in the electric coffee percolator. "But I mean, wouldn't divorce be a good idea? Then you could move back to London."

"I need proof. I need good, solid proof that he's been messing about and then I can take him to the cleaner's."

"Don't you have any money of your own?"

"No." A bitter little no.

"What did you do before you were married?"

"I modelled. Not top-flight or even the second landing. Catalogue stuff, TV ads for sanitary towels, that sort of thing."

"How did you meet Tolly?" Agatha took down two mugs and took out the milk and sugar.

"At an Ideal Home Exhibition. Me and another model were hired to wear bath towels and decorate his stand. He took me out for dinner, and that was that."

Agatha poured two cups of coffee. "Help yourself to milk and sugar." She lit a cigarette.

"Mind if I have one of those?" asked Lucy.

"Sure." Agatha pushed the packet forward. "I thought you didn't smoke.

Couldn't see any ashtrays in that house of yours."

"Tolly won't let me. He used to smoke sixty a day."

"Oh, one of those. How long have you been married?"

"Five years."

"Five years? Were you married before?"

"Not me." Lucy shrugged. "Always waiting for Mr. Right. Anyway, the reason I called is this. I want you to get proof for me of his philandering. You said you were a detective. I've got some money squirrelled away. I'll pay you."

"It's not the sort of thing I like to do," said Agatha slowly. "Messy and dirty business."

Lucy surveyed her impatiently. "What else have you got to do in this God-alive place where they believe in fairies?"

"I'm writing a book." Agatha had forgotten until then about her book. She was suddenly eager to get back to it.

"Think about it," urged Lucy. "I'm desperate."

"I tell you what, I'll ask around," said Agatha. "A few of the women here seem bitter about Rosie."

If I did a bit more investigating, thought Agatha, it would be good for the book. It's based on this unlovely couple anyway.

Her mind returned to the fairies. "Any children in this village?" she asked.

"A few. Not many young couples, so the others have children who are grown up and married and living elsewhere. There isn't a council house estate here, so no young mothers. Betty Jackson, over in the cottage beyond the estate agent's, has four, but like all kids these days, after they get bussed back from school, they're usually stuck in front of the television set."

"I wonder how whoever it is gets in houses so easily to take stuff?"

"A lot of people don't lock their doors, or they leave the key under the doormat or on a string hanging through the letter-box. Forget about fairies, Agatha. Try to get something on Tolly."

After she had left, Agatha decided to go back to writing her book. Determined not to read a word of it until she had completed one chapter, she ploughed on. It was only when the light started fading outside that she realized she was ferociously hungry and that she had promised to meet the women at the pub.

She put a frozen curry in the microwave, and when it was ready, ate it quickly and went up to change her clothes.

The pub was relatively empty. Harriet, Amy, and Polly were there with their husbands. When Agatha showed signs of joining them, Henry Freemantle gave her a venomous glare. No one offered to buy her a drink.

Agatha was suddenly fed up with the lot of them. "What can I get you, Mrs. Raisin?" asked Rosie Wilden. Her blond hair was piled up on her head, apart from one errant curl straying down to a creamy bosom, almost down to the nipple exposed by another plunging blouse, black this time.

"A bottle of arsenic," said Agatha sourly.

Rosie let out a peal of laughter. "You are a one."

"Aren't I?" said Agatha. "Are you having an affair with Tolly Trumpington-James?"

Rosie's good humour was undented. "Mrs. Raisin, dear, according to the local gossip, I'm having a affair with every man in this village. Tolly don't even come in here. Too common for him."

"I think I'll change my mind about ordering a drink," said Agatha. "I don't want to go and sit with that lot."

"Suit yourself. Sit somewhere else?"

"No, tell them I've left something in the oven."

Agatha made her escape, walking straight

past the table where her new friends and their husbands were sitting.

This time, she remembered to pick up her car. She drove home. Her cats were in the garden. They came in on stiff legs, backs arched, fur standing out. Agatha looked down at them. Then she looked down the garden. Those lights were dancing around again.

With a roar of rage, she ran down the garden. The lights flickered and disappeared.

She ran back into the house and through it and out to her car, where she got a torch.

Then she hurried back to the garden again and began to search every inch of ground where she had seen those lights. The grass was springy and uncut, being a wild area beyond the drying green which Barry had mowed.

Baffled, she returned to the house. She took out the inventory and began to check everything carefully. Nothing seemed to be missing.

But she felt frightened and uneasy.

THREE

†

The bad weather Agatha had seen approaching had arrived by the following morning. Agatha awoke to the sounds of howling wind and rain pattering against the windows. She dressed and went downstairs. The house was cold.

She went into the sitting-room. With sunlight streaming in the windows, it had seemed tastefully furnished, the sofa and chairs upholstered in checked tweed, the carpet a warm burnt orange. But now it appeared what it was, a room in a rented cottage with ornaments on the mantelpiece that she would never have bought and pictures that she would never have hung.

She lit the fire. Must get more fire-lighters, she thought. Agatha used half a packet to light a fire. When the logs were crackling merrily, she went into the kitchen and made herself a coffee and carried it back to the sitting-room.

Agatha felt lost and alien. She rose after a while and went to the phone in the hall. Must get an extension and put it in the sitting-room, she vowed. Silly to have to stand in a cold hall. She phoned Mrs. Bloxby. "Oh, it's you," said the vicar's wife. "No, he isn't back yet."

"I'm not phoning about that," said Agatha crossly. "I might come back earlier than I intended."

"It'll be nice to see you. But, why? Has anything suddenly gone wrong?"

"It's a bit boring and it's started to rain." Not for a moment would Agatha admit that the fairy lights had frightened her. Such as Agatha Raisin was frightened of so many things — love, confrontations, aging, living alone — that she went at life with both fists metaphorically swinging.

"You're near Norwich, aren't you?" asked Mrs. Bloxby in her gentle voice.

"Not far, no."

"Might be an idea to go and see a silly movie and look at the shops."

This was an eminently sensible idea, but Agatha felt cross. She wanted Mrs. Bloxby to say that everyone in Carsely missed her and beg her to come home.

74

"I'll think about it," she said sourly. "Any news your end?"

"Miss Simms has a new boyfriend." Miss Simms was Carsely's unmarried mother and secretary of the ladies' society.

"Really?" Agatha was momentarily diverted. "Who?"

"He's something in carpets. She gave me one of those fake Chinese rugs. So kind."

"I can't imagine you putting a fake Chinese rug in your sitting-room."

"It's in Alf's study. It's got a stone floor and his feet get cold when he's writing his sermons, so it's ideal."

"Anything else?"

"The Red Lion is being threatened with redecoration."

"Why? I like it the way it is," said Agatha, thinking fondly of the low-beamed pub and its comfortable shabby chairs.

"It's not John Fletcher's idea. It's the brewery. I think they want it art deco."

"But that's dreadful, and so old-hat," screeched Agatha. "You've got to get up a protest."

"We have."

"Maybe I'd better come back and really get things going."

"You aren't listening. The ladies' society has already collected signatures from everyone in the village. I don't think the brewery will go ahead in the face of such protest."

"No, I don't suppose they will," said Agatha in a small voice.

"Lovely weather, isn't it?"

"It's pissing down with rain here."

Agatha coloured as a short, reproving silence greeted the profanity. Then Mrs. Bloxby said, "Perhaps you should consider coming back. I know the winters can be bad here, but they're truly dreadful in Norfolk."

Agatha seized on the invitation like a lifeline. "I'll probably be back next week."

After she had said goodbye, she felt better. Now for some coffee and that book.

Unfortunately, she decided to start off by printing out what she had written and reading it. "What a load of waffle," she groaned. "It's not *literary* enough." How the hell could you get a book on friends' coffee tables or get the Booker Prize if you didn't write literature?

She frowned. Of course, she could always start again and write one of those stream-of-consciousness novels with an eff as every second word. But she wasn't from Glasgow and all the successful effers seemed to come from Glasgow. Or there was the literary trick of observing the minutiae of surroundings. Literary writers always ended up lying in the grass describing each blade and insect.

Agatha looked gloomily out of the window at the driving rain. Fat chance of lying in grass in this weather.

She switched off the computer and stood up. What to do? No use investigating the infidelity of Tolly. Agatha was sure Rose Wilden had been telling the truth.

The doorbell rang. Agatha opened it. Harriet stood on the step, sheltering under an enormous golfing umbrella.

Agatha invited her in. Harriet left her umbrella and waxed coat in the hall. "I came to thank you," she said.

"What for?"

"Believe it or not, Rosie came up to our table last night and went on about how nice it was to see ladies in the pub. Our husbands were so disappointed."

"Your husband came here and threatened me."

"He's got a lousy temper and he really did have a bad crush on Rosie. But now that's gone."

"Good. So he and the others will stay home in the evenings?"

"No, they're going to find a pub in another village."

"So we didn't achieve anything."

"Oh, yes, we did. At least we know none of

our husbands is going to have an affair with Rosie."

Agatha thought about the husbands — Harriet's, tall, thin and pompous; Polly's, small, round and pompous; Amy's, small and ferrety — and opened her mouth to say it was her considered opinion that none of their husbands had the slightest chance of bedding Rosie, but uncharacteristically held her tongue. She clung on to the fact that she would soon be leaving Fryfam and its fairies.

Instead she asked, "What on earth do you do in Fryfam on a day like this?"

"There's always household chores to catch up on. Then there's church-cleaning duty. It's my day for the brasses."

"Talking about cleaning, I'd better get someone for here," said Agatha, thinking she'd better leave it as clean as she had found it.

"There's Mrs. Jackson. I'll write down her phone number for you if you've got a bit of paper."

"Thanks." Agatha found a piece of paper. Harriet was writing down the number when the bell rang again. When Agatha opened the door it was to find Polly there.

"Come and join us," she said. "Harriet's here."

Polly took off a large yellow oilskin coat and sou'wester. "Gosh, what a day! Such excitement!"

She followed Agatha into the kitchen. "You'll never guess. There's been a theft up at the manor."

"Never!" said Harriet. "Oh, I know. Is it those lights again?"

"Yes, Tolly saw them at the back of the manor, but he was convinced it was kids playing tricks."

"So what's been pinched?" asked Agatha, "The usual piece of tat?"

"No," said Polly. "You'll never believe. . . . Any chance of coffee?"

"Right away," said Agatha. "But go on. What was nicked?"

"A Stubbs."

"Never!" exclaimed Harriet.

Agatha did not want to ask what a Stubbs was and so betray her ignorance, but curiosity overcame her.

"Stubbs?" she asked.

"George Stubbs," said Harriet. "An eighteenth-century painter, famous for his paintings of horses. Must be worth a mint."

"Where was it?" asked Agatha. "Didn't see anything like that in their drawing-room."

"It was in Tolly's study," said Polly.

79

"So how did they get in?"

"That's the mystery," said Polly, bobbing up and down on her chair in excitement. "Before Tolly does the rounds, he locks up everything and sets the burglar alarm."

Agatha poured mugs of coffee and bent down to ferret in a cupboard for a packet of biscuits. "So what are the police doing?" she asked, straightening up and crackling open a packet of chocolate digestives.

"The CID and forensic people are all over the place. That lazy policeman, Framp, has been told to stand guard all night."

"Seems a bit silly now the robbery has taken place."

"That's what Framp says. Oh, Agatha, if the press come round, you mustn't say anything about fairies," said Polly.

"Why not?"

"Because we'd all be a laughing-stock."

Agatha put the biscuits on a plate and put them down on the table. "So why do you believe in the things in the first place? I mean, surely you two don't."

"There's odd things in this area. It's very old," said Harriet.

"But, come on," protested Agatha. "Fairies!"

"So if you're so clever," said Polly, "what's your explanation?"

"Someone fooling about. Gets superstitious people scared, steals rubbish, then goes in for the kill. What's a Stubbs worth?"

"I've heard Tolly bragging it was insured for one million pounds," said Harriet.

"Blimey!"

"Lucy's freaked out," said Polly with relish. "She says she's clearing off to London to stay with a couple of friends."

Another ring at the doorbell. "I suppose that's Amy." Agatha went to answer it as Harriet called after her, "Can't be Amy. She's working."

Agatha swung open the door. "Charles!" she cried. She had forgotten all about telling Mrs. Bloxby to pass on her address and phone number to him.

Rain was trickling down from his well-groomed hair. In one hand, he carried a large suitcase. "Can I come in, Aggie?" he asked plaintively.

"Yes, sure. Leave your stuff in the hall. I've got company, but they'll be leaving in a minute." Charles dumped his suitcase and struggled out of his raincoat. "What weather. It was sunshine all the way until I got to the county border."

"We're in the kitchen," said Agatha, hoping that a friendship with a baronet would cancel out her ignorance of George Stubbs.

She introduced Charles. Her triumph was short-lived. "Your nephew?" asked Harriet.

"Just a friend," snapped Agatha. Charles was in his forties and she was in her fifties — but a very *well-preserved* fifties.

"We must go." Harriet and Polly got to their feet. "I'll show you out." Agatha's face was sour. It would be a long time, she felt, before she forgave Harriet for mistaking Charles for her nephew.

When she had slammed the door behind them, Agatha peered at her face in the hall mirror and let out a squawk of alarm. She did not have on any make-up and her hair was a mess.

"Be down in a minute," she called to Charles. "Help yourself to coffee."

She darted up to her bedroom, and sitting down at the dressing-table, applied a thin film of some anti-aging cream and then a light foundation. Powder, lipstick, but no eye shadow — too early in the day. She brushed her thick brown hair until it shone and then returned downstairs, where Charles was sitting on the kitchen floor, playing with the cats.

"You might have phoned first," said Agatha.

"Came on impulse." Charles jumped lightly to his feet and dusted himself down.

He was such a clean man, thought Agatha. His shirt was immaculate, his trousers pressed, his shoes gleaming. Even naked, he never looked vulnerable but as if he were wearing a neat white suit.

"How long are you staying?"

"Depends," said Charles, stifling a yawn. "What goes on in this burg?"

"Lots," said Agatha. "Take your case up to the spare room. That's the one with the *single* bed."

"Okay."

Charles disappeared. I should have told him I was only going to stay another week, thought Agatha. Oh, well, a week of Charles will be enough. And I am not going to bed with him, ever again. But it certainly looks as if things in Fryfam are getting very interesting indeed.

When Charles came down again, he found Agatha looking at ready meals from the freezer. "Back to the microwave, eh?" said Charles. "Last time I saw you, you had gone in for real food."

"This is real food," snapped Agatha. "Just because I don't cook it doesn't mean it isn't real. I bet you most of the stuff you get in those restaurants you go to is ready-made and supplied by some catering firm. I know a restaurant in Moreton-in-Marsh that's pulled in all sorts of awards and yet someone who worked there told me that everything from duck à l'orange to boeuf stroganoff comes in a boil-in-bag. What about haddock in a cheese sauce?"

"Why not?" Charles sat down at the table. "Now what's going on here?"

As she worked at her domestic chores of taking off cardboard wrappings, piercing cling film and popping packets in the microwave, Agatha told him about the fairies of Fryfam and the theft of the Stubbs.

"But no murder?" asked Charles. "I always see you surrounded by dead bodies."

"Don't," said Agatha with a shudder. "Although there's a bit more. Tolly's wife thinks he's having an affair with Rosie Wilden, who runs the local pub, but she denies it and I believe her."

"Why?" mocked Charles. "Is she that ugly?"

"On the contrary, she's a country beauty."

"Aha, let's skip the frozen fish and go to the pub."

"They don't do meals."

"What? Not even a Scotch egg?"

"Not even that. It's like a man's club or an old-fashioned pub. Women not welcome while the men gawp at Rosie."

Charles looked around him. "Not bad for a rented cottage. Bit cold, though."

"No central heating. Lots of logs and I'll light this Calor gas heater."

"What on earth brought you here?"

"Just an impulse. I was bored and I stuck a pin in the map."

She put a plate of fish in front of Charles. "Any wine?" he asked.

"I've got a bottle of Chablis I got in Tesco's the other day."

"Tesco's around here?"

"Norwich." Agatha took the bottle out of the fridge and handed him an opener.

"That reminds me," she said, "the night I arrived I went down to the pub looking for food. Rosie said they didn't do meals but invited me through to the kitchen to have some of the family food, which was delicious. She gave me this wine which was marvellous. I didn't know what it was."

"So why didn't you ask her?"

"I meant to. But then it went out of my mind. I was taken aback when she wouldn't let me pay for anything. I've been invited to join the women's group here. I've been quilting."

Charles snorted with laughter. "Poor you. You must have been at your wits' end for some amusement. So let's finish this and go out and visit Tolly Trumpington-James."

"There'll be police all over the place and Lucy's cleared off to London."

"Still, we shall turn our great brains to the task of the missing Stubbs."

The rain had settled down to a dismal drizzle. "Not much of a place," commented Charles as they drove past the village green.

"Looks all right in the sunshine."

They drove out to the manor house. Various police cars, vans and other cars were parked outside.

They went up. Agatha rang the bell. The door was opened by the grumpy-looking woman who had served tea the day before.

"Tell Mr. Trumpington-James I wish to see him," said Agatha grandly.

She clumped off. After a few moments, she returned and said, "He's too busy."

The door began to close. Charles held out his card. "I'm staying with Mrs. Raisin. Perhaps he would like to give me a call?"

She squinted down at the card and the legend "Sir Charles Fraith."

Tolly appeared in the hall behind. "She gone yet?" he called.

The surly woman said. "She's got a Sir Charles Fraith with her."

Tolly surged forward, pushing her aside,

an unctuous smile on his face.

"Glad to see you, Sir Charles," he said. "Come in. Come for some hunting? You do ride on horseback?"

"Camel, actually," said Charles.

Tolly goggled at him, and then burst out laughing. "Joke, eh? That's a good one. Come through. Mind if I call you Charles?"

He strode off in the direction of the drawing-room. "What a twat," muttered Charles. "Come on, Aggie."

They went into the drawing-room. "Heard you'd had a painting pinched," said Charles. "Insured, I hope?"

"Fortunately. But it's not the money that bothers me. It's the fact that some cheeky bugger walked into my house as cool as you please and took it off the wall and disappeared with it."

"And the burglar alarm was set?" asked Agatha.

"Yes," said Tolly impatiently, "and all the doors and windows were locked."

"It was taken from the study, wasn't it. Can we have a look?"

"Not now. The police are in there."

"What about that woman who answered the door?"

"Betty Jackson. Yes. But she's salt of the earth."

"I find her a grumpy old bitch," said Agatha.

Tolly stared insolently at her. "You wouldn't understand. People like us are used to servants, eh Charles?"

"No," said Charles. "I get women up from the village to clean and when I've got a big house party, I get a catering company to cope. Aggie's quite right, you know. She *is* a grumpy old bitch."

Tolly let out false bray of laughter. Then he said, "Plan to stay long? I belong to the local hunt. Got some good hunting around here."

"Don't hunt," said Charles.

Tolly eyed him with sudden suspicion. "What did you get your knighthood for?"

"It's a baronetcy," said Charles patiently. "In the family for years."

"And where's your place?"

"Warwickshire. Actually, the reason we called is that Aggie and I have made a pretty good job at solving some mysteries in the past. Thought we might be able to help you."

"Very kind of you. I don't see what you can do that the police can't."

The door of the drawing-room opened, and a nondescript man looked in. "Could we have a word with you, sir?"

"Sure." He turned to Agatha and Charles. "This is Detective Chief Inspector Percy Hand. He's in charge of things. I've been talking to a couple of amateur detectives here."

Hand gave them a bleak smile. "If you could come with me, sir."

"Right," said Tolly. "Come again, if you like. Can you see yourselves out?"

"What a pill," marvelled Charles. "It's a wonder it's not a murder we're looking at."

They got in the car. "What's up, Aggie? You've got a face like a fiddle."

"Why the hell should he think I'm not one of their sort! That's what he said." Agatha looked miserably at her hands.

"Oh, that. It's because he's a vulgar pushy little man, insecure socially and always trying to put someone down. Cheer up. Maybe someone will murder him and then life around here will really get exciting."

Agatha found she was enjoying Charles's company. They took a walk in the rain in the late afternoon. The air was full of the smell of grass and plants, although over all hung the redolent scent of the pine trees. They walked down past the little row of shops, farther than Agatha had gone, and turning a corner, found there were more little shops around the bend: an ironmonger's, a thrift shop, a dried-flower shop, which also sold candles of all shapes and sizes, and a small garage with two rusting old cars at the side of the forecourt.

The drizzle was steady and soaking and began to sweep across their vision in curtains of rain blown by a rising wind. Night had fallen and lights twinkled in cottage windows.

"Pub should be open by now," said Charles. "Let's go for a drink."

The pub was still empty. Agatha took a seat by the fire after removing her soaking raincoat. "A gin and tonic for me, Charles."

Charles went up and rapped on the bar. A strong waft of rose perfume heralded the arrival of Rosie Wilden in a cream wool dress which complemented the creaminess of her complexion and the vivid blue of her eyes.

Charles leaned over the bar and began to flirt. First he affected astonishment that such rare beauty could be found behind the bar of a village pub. Then he began to ask her about herself. It was when he got around to asking her if she ever had a night off that Agatha called crossly, "What about my drink, Charles?"

"Right," he called back but without turning around. "That'll be a gin and tonic and a half of bitter."

Then he fumbled in his jacket. "I'm afraid I've forgotten my wallet."

"That's all right, sir. I'll put it on the slate."

"No need for that. Aggie'll pay. Aggie?"

Agatha marched up to the bar and put the money on the counter. "Why don't you come and join me, Charles?" she demanded. "Or are you going to prop up the bar all night?"

Charles sat down opposite her and said, "The way you go on sometimes, one would think we were married."

"Particularly when you never pay for anything."

"Well, she's quite something."

Agatha felt all the irritation any woman feels when her escort praises some other woman. "I'd forgotten what you were like." Agatha sighed. "In fact, I've made a mistake coming here. I'm going back home next week."

"What, with fairies shining lights and a Stubbs stolen? Not like you. Where's your curiosity?"

"It first got washed away in the rain and then, when you said you'd forgotten your wallet, I realized your company was not going to alleviate the boredom."

"Nasty!"

"But so true." The firelight flickered on Charles's well-barbered neat features. Oh, why couldn't it be James sitting opposite?

The pub began to fill up. Agatha saw the three husbands come in, Henry, Jerry and Peter, minus wives.

Jerry was complaining about PC Framp. "I'm glad that lazy hound of a copper has to stand out in the rain all night outside the manor. Mind you, it's a case of bolting the stable door after the horse has fled. I hope he gets pneumonia. I've never forgiven him for that time he pulled me over on the Norwich Road because one of my brake lights was out. He refused to let me drive on and I had to get a cab home."

"Yes, you told us . . . many times," commented Peter Dart, leering at Rosie.

"What a waste of champagne," said Agatha, half to herself. "I haven't done any good there at all."

"What?" asked Charles. "What are you muttering about?"

"Those three men at the bar neglect their wives to come in here and goggle at Rosie. So I brought the wives in and threw a champagne party. They told me their husbands were going to find another pub, but there they are again. Do you think Rosie is really innocent? Do you think she flirts?"

"I think when a woman looks like Rosie, she doesn't need to flirt. And what are you doing interfering in village marriages? No wonder murders follow you around."

Agatha felt a spasm of dislike for Charles. "Let's go," she said. "I'm bored."

They had a supper of microwaved curry. Charles settled down to watch television. Agatha had forgotten that he had a tremendous appetite for rubbishy television. She said crossly that she was going to bed but he was watching a movie called *Monsters of the Dark* and did not hear her.

Agatha went grumpily up to bed. She stared at her face in the bathroom mirror. The rain had washed all her make-up off. She felt old and unattractive. She had a leisurely bath. Then she climbed into bed, propped herself up on the pillows and looked through the selection of paperbacks she had placed on the bedside table. She had bought a selection of light reading. There was a large blockbuster which claimed to be, according to the blurb, "erotic and unputdownable." Agatha flicked through it. Gucci labels and crumpled bedsheets. The next came under the category of chick-fic, or rather one of those women's books, a romance clothed in a convoluted literary style. She discarded that. The next was an Aga saga, a novel set in a village where a well-heeled middle-aged woman found out her husband was unfaithful to her. Agatha was very much of her roots and found it hard to believe that anyone who had money in the bank could suffer in the same way as someone poor. She often felt her yearning for James was ridiculous. She put that aside and settled for a hard cop novel set in the deep southern states of the United States. After a few pages the book slipped from her hand.

Charles came into her room later to say good night. He switched out her bedside light and kissed her on the forehead. Agatha stirred and muttered something but did not wake.

She was dreaming of James. They were on a Mediterranean cruise. She could feel the sun on her cheek. They were leaning against the rail. James turned and smiled down at her. "Agatha," he said.

"Agatha! Agatha!" In her dream, Agatha wondered why James was suddenly shouting at her. Then she woke up with a start, realizing it was morning and someone was banging at the door downstairs and shouting her name.

She pulled on a dressing-gown and hurried down the stairs, nearly tripping over the cats, who snaked around her ankles.

She wrenched open the door. Amy Worth stood there, her eyes dilated with excitement.

"What's up?" asked Agatha sleepily.

"It's Tolly. You'll never believe it."

"Believe what?"

"He's dead . . . murdered . . . and with Framp guarding the house, too!"

FOUR

✝

Charles came down the stairs in his dressing gown. "What's all the row about, darling?" he called.

"Come in, Amy," said Agatha, flushing with embarrassment. She said to Charles, "Tolly's been murdered."

"How? When?"

"Last night," said Amy. "I don't know yet how he was killed. Betty Jackson, the cleaner, went up to the manor this morning and let herself in."

"So she has a key?" asked Charles.

"Yes, and she can operate the burglar alarm. It was still on! She said she went upstairs to see if anyone was at home and she found Tolly dead on the landing."

"Maybe he knew who had stolen that painting of his."

"Insurance prices, as a rule," said Charles, "are often twice or three times the auction estimate. Unless Tolly was so filthy rich he didn't care, I would have thought he would have been delighted to get the insurance money. How much was it insured for?"

"Tolly told everyone he had insured it for a million."

They sat down round the kitchen table.

"A Stubbs," mused Charles. "Now what would a man like Tolly be doing having a Stubbs?"

"I can explain that," said Amy, her face pink with excitement and the importance at being the source of so much interesting gossip. "It was just after they moved down here. Lord Tarrymundy was visiting friends in Norfolk and came over for a day's hunting. Of course, he impressed poor Tolly no end, him being a lord and all. The next thing he says a gentleman like Tolly should start collecting and offered to sell him the Stubbs, knock-down price, he said. I believe it was three hundred and thirty thousand pounds, which isn't really a knock-down price, but Tolly bought it and then insured it high. But this is the thing. At that time, they had a house in Launceston Place in Kensington. Lucy adored it. Evidently when they were first married, they held very chic parties there. Tolly ups and says they can't afford two residences and he's happy in the country and sells the house for nearly a million. Poor Lucy was furious."

"Can one make a fortune from bathroom showers?" asked Charles.

"Evidently," said Amy eagerly. "He sold all over the world, or so he says, and sold the business to an American company."

"So," said Agatha slowly, "Lucy would hardly steal the painting and then murder her husband. I mean, all she had to do was murder him and then she would get everything, Stubbs and all."

"But she was in London when the murder took place," exclaimed Amy. "So it can't be anything to do with her at all."

"Who's the handsome fellow at the bottom of your garden, Agatha?" asked Charles. "Not a fairy?"

"No, that's Barry Jones, who does the garden."

"I wonder if he does any gardening up at the manor," said Charles.

"I'll ask him." Agatha opened the back door and called, "Barry?"

The gardener walked up to the back door and entered the kitchen, doffing his cap to reveal a thick head of chestnut hair. He had the same bright blue eyes as Rosie Wilden. He was wearing a shirt with the sleeves cut off and his bronzed and muscled arms were a miracle of human sculpture.

"We're talking about the murder of Tolly," said Agatha. "Do you garden up at the manor?"

"I did, missus, for a while. No flowers or vegetables, but he likes the lawns kept trim. Then, three weeks ago, he sacks me. I says to him, 'Is my work unsatisfactory?' And he says, 'I want a real gardener. Going to get the place landscaped.'"

"Do you know how he was killed?" asked Charles.

"No, but Mrs. Jackson is telling everyone that Mrs. Raisin and her boyfriend were the last to see him alive, so I reckon the police'll be calling on you soon enough."

"Thanks, Barry. You can go back to work. I'd better get dressed. You, too, Charles."

Agatha had only just finished dressing when the doorbell went again. She ran downstairs and opened the door to the man she remembered as Detective Inspector Percy Hand. He was accompanied by another detective.

"You are Mrs. Raisin?" he asked.

"Yes, come in. It's about this murder?"

She led both men into the sitting-room. The sun was shining again, streaming through the windows to light up the debris of Charles's night-time television viewing — coffee-cup, biscuit packet and TV Guide.

"Sit down," said Agatha. "Coffee?"

"Thank you."

Agatha called up the stairs on her road to the kitchen, "Hurry up, Charles. The police are here."

As she plugged in the percolator, she suddenly remembered the manuscript of *Death at the Manor* lying on the desk in the sitting-room. The desk was in a dark corner. Surely he wouldn't prowl around looking at things.

The coffee seemed to take ages to percolate. Where was Charles? He should be doing this and giving her the opportunity to get that manuscript. At last she poured two mugs of coffee and put them on a tray along with milk and sugar and a plate of biscuits.

She walked into the sitting room, carrying the tray — and nearly dropped it. Hand was standing at the desk flicking through her manuscript.

"Aren't you supposed to have a search warrant before you go poking through my things?" asked Agatha harshly.

"We can get one," said Hand, looking at her mildly. "I find it interesting that your book is called *Death at the Manor*, and here we have a death at the manor."

"Coincidence," snapped Agatha, setting the tray down on the coffee-table.

"A lot of coincidence," he murmured. "This is Detective Sergeant Carey." And to Agatha's rage, he handed Carey the manuscript, saying, "Have a look at this."

Charles came in at that moment and Agatha hailed him with a furious cry of "Charles, they're reading my book and they don't have a search warrant."

"I didn't know you were writing a book," said Charles. "Still, you lot are being a bit cheeky."

"Mrs. Raisin's book is called *Death at the Manor*," said Hand.

Charles laughed. "Oh, Aggie, your first attempt at writing?"

Agatha nodded.

Charles turned to Hand. "How was Tolly murdered?"

"His throat was cut with a razor."

"You mean, one of those old-fashioned cutthroat razors?"

"Exactly. And in Mrs. Raisin's manuscript, the owner of the manor, Peregrine Pickle, is murdered when someone slits his throat."

"You can't call him Peregrine Pickle," said Charles, momentarily diverted.

"Why not?"

"It's the title of a book by Tobias Smollett. A classic, Aggie."

"I can change the name." Agatha turned red. She hated the gaps in her education being pointed out. "But what on earth are we doing discussing literary points? They've got no right to look at anything of mine without my permission."

"She is right, you know," said Charles.

There was a ring at the doorbell. "That'll be for us," said Hand. He went to the door and came back waving a piece of paper. "Now, this is a search warrant, Mrs. Raisin. Before I get my men in, I would like to ask you some questions."

Agatha sat down on the sofa next to Charles, defeated. Her outrage at the detectives looking at her manuscript was not because she was furious at the intrusion, but because she was ashamed of her work.

She and Charles answered the preliminary questions: who they were, where they came from, what they were doing in Fryfam.

"So we get to what you were both doing at the manor yesterday," said Hand. "Mr. Trumpington-James said something about the pair of you being amateur detectives."

Before Charles could stop her, Agatha, nervous, had launched into a full brag of all the cases she had solved. Charles saw the cynical glances the detectives exchanged and knew they were putting Agatha down as a slightly unbalanced eccentric.

"I think at the moment," said Hand sarcastically, when Agatha's voice had finally trailed off under his stony stare, "that we'll just settle for good old-fashioned police work. But should we find ourselves baffled, we will appeal to you for help. Can we go on? Right. Why did you visit Mr. Trumpington-James? Had either of you known him before you came here? You first, Mrs. Raisin."

Agatha described how she had first been invited for tea. Then she hesitated a moment, wondering whether to tell Hand about Lucy's suspicions of her husband's infidelity. Then she thought angrily, why should I? Let him find out for himself if he's so damned clever.

"You hesitated there," said Hand. "Is there something you're holding back?"

"No," said Agatha. "Why should I hold anything back?"

Hand turned to Charles. "You say you did not know Mr. Trumpington-James before and yet you called on him with Mrs. Raisin. Why? You only arrived yesterday."

"Aggie told me about the theft of the Stubbs."

"Aggie being Mrs. Raisin."

"It's Agatha, actually," said Agatha crossly.

"So, Sir Charles, you called. Why?"

Charles felt ashamed of saying they thought they might be able to find out who had stolen the Stubbs after all Agatha's bragging, but he shrugged and said, "We thought we might get an idea of who had taken it."

"How?" demanded Hand sharply. He should cut his fingernails, thought Agatha. They're like claws, all chalky and ridged.

"How, what?"

"How on earth did you think, Sir Charles, that you could find out something the police could not? You do not have forensic equipment or even a knowledge of the area."

"I know you didn't believe Agatha when she was going on about the mysteries she solved," said Charles patiently, "but you can always check with the Mircester police. You see, people talk to us the way they wouldn't talk to a policeman, and I'll tell you why. Take you, for instance. By sneering at Aggie, you put her back up, so if by any chance she does hear a useful piece of gossip, she won't go running to you."

"If I find either of you have been withholding useful evidence, then I shall charge you."

"Just listen to yourself," said Charles, un-flustered. "Now you've put my back up."

"We will start our search now," said Hand grimly. "And we will be keeping this manuscript for the moment. You will get a receipt for it."

After two hours, the police left. "I'm starving," said Charles. "We haven't had breakfast. Got eggs?"

"Yes."

"I'll make us an omelette and then we'll go and see that copper, the local bod; what's his name?"

"Framp."

"That's the one."

"But why him, Charles?"

"Because he's only a copper and I'll bet he got the wrong side of Hand's mouth. We'll go and be oh, so sympathetic."

"Won't he be up at the manor?"

"Not him. He'll have been sent back to his beat with a flea between both ears. I'll make that omelette."

Agatha sat hunched over a mug of coffee in the kitchen, watching Charles as he whisked eggs in a bowl. Why do I always land up with men who never tell me what they really think of me? she wondered. Charles had made love to her in the past but he had never said anything particularly affectionate. He came and went in her life, leaving very little trace of his real thoughts or personality.

After they had eaten, they headed out to see PC Framp. Agatha said testily — cross because Charles had insisted they walk and she was wearing high heels — that it was a useless effort. PC Framp would at least have been roped in to comb the bushes around the manor for clues.

There was a high wind which sent the tops of the pine trees tossing and making a sound like the sea, but on the ground it was strangely calm, apart from sudden whispering puffs of wind. Little snakes of sandy soil blew from the roots of the trees and writhed across the road at their feet. Not only were Agatha's shoes high-heeled but they had thin straps at the front of each and gritty bits of sand were working their way inside her tights and along the soles of her feet.

"There's his car!" said Charles triumphantly as they approached the police station.

They rang the bell and waited. No reply. "Let's try round the back," said Charles.

They walked along the side of the building and through a low wooden gate that led into the back garden. Framp could be seen standing over a smoking oil drum burning leaves he had raked up from the grass.

"Off duty," he called when they saw him.

Undeterred, Charles went up to him. "You know Mrs. Raisin here. I'm Charles Fraith."

"I heard of you. You were at the manor yesterday," said Framp. An erratic gust of wind sent smoke swirling into his eyes and he rubbed them with the back of one grimy hand.

"I'm surprised a bright copper like you isn't on the job," pursued Charles, "what with all this murder and robbery."

"Told to go about my regular duties," said Framp sulkily. "You would think it was my fault he was murdered. I was on duty all night outside that house and I never heard a sound. No one came or went."

"So who do you think did it?"

"Let's have a cup of tea." Framp gave the smoldering leaves a vicious poke with a rusty metal rod. Little tongues of flame licked round the leaves and more aromatic smoke filled the air.

They followed him into his messy kitchen. A kettle was already simmering on an old iron stove. He put five tea-bags into a small teapot, stirred it up, and poured each of them mugs of black tea.

He sat down wearily at the table. "You ask who did it? It's the wife, for sure."

"But I gather she was in London," said Agatha.

"So she says, and anyway, her alibi hasn't been checked out yet and even if it is, her friends could lie for her."

"Why her?" asked Charles.

"She hated it here. Wanted to go to London. So she pinches the painting first, bumps him off, knowing she'll inherit everything along with the insurance money. She can't sell the painting, everyone will be on the look-out for it. Anyway, it was insured for a mint, so it's worth more to her lost."

"I didn't like Hand," said Agatha. "Unpleasant sort of man."

"Nobody likes him," said Framp gloomily. He stifled a yawn. "I'd better get some sleep."

"Where's Lucy Trumpington-James at the moment?" asked Agatha.

"Arriving by police car from London any moment."

"Mrs. Jackson knows how to operate the burglar alarm, doesn't she?"

"Yes, but come on. She's a villager and lived here all her life."

"Is there a Mr. Jackson?" asked Charles.

"Yes, but he's doing time in the Scrubs."

"Wormwood Scrubs? Prison?"

"That's the one."

"What for?" asked Agatha.

"Robbery with violence. Beat a guard at a warehouse nearly to death. Got fifteen years. Not for so much beating the guard. This is Britain, after all. For stealing eighteen thousand pounds."

"When was this?" asked Agatha.

"Two years ago."

"So that lets him out. Did they find the money?"

"Yes; he wasn't living with his wife at the time. They found the lot in a flat in Clapham in London."

"And was this his first crime?"

"First major one. Before that, lots of petty stuff, car hijacking, that sort of thing."

"Where does Mrs. Jackson live?"

"Why?" demanded Framp sharply.

"I need a cleaner," said Agatha patiently, "and she'll have spare time at the moment, with the police being all over the manor. By the way, does the manor house have a name?"

"Reckon folks have always just called it the manor."

Charles took another sip of bitter black tea and repressed a shudder. "We'd better get on our way, Aggie."

"That what they call you?" asked Framp with a momentary flash of humour. "You don't look like an Aggie to me."

"It's Agatha, actually." She threw a baleful look at Charles and then turned back to Framp. "So where does Mrs. Jackson live?"

"You know Short's garage?"

"We saw it yesterday."

"Well, her cottage is tucked in the back of that."

"Let's get the car," pleaded Agatha once they were out on the road again.

"Why not just go home and put on a pair of flat walking shoes? People might stop and talk to us on our way there. You can't pick up gossip if you're flashing past in a car."

"Oh, okay," said Agatha, although she felt that wearing flats made her look dumpy.

When they set out again, Agatha began to wonder what villagers they were supposed to meet. The village green was deserted.

They walked across it and down the street past the estate agent's, where Amy could be seen crouched over a computer. Then Agatha saw Carrie Smiley and Polly Dart approaching and greeted them with "Isn't it terrible about Tolly?"

"Terrible," echoed Carrie. "Have the

police been to see you?"

"Yes," said Agatha. "They have, as a matter of fact. Did you expect them to?"

"Oh, yes," said Carrie. "It's all round the village that you were probably the last person to see him alive."

"Then it's just as well his throat was cut in the middle of the night," said Agatha. "I say, it *was* the middle of the night?"

"Nobody knows," barked Polly. "But the police didn't leave until late last night, leaving only Framp on duty. The press have arrived. Such excitement!"

"Where are they?"

"In the pub. Rosie opened up especially early the minute she heard about the murder. She says the press always drink a lot. Where are you off to?"

"To see Mrs. Jackson. I need someone to clean. I don't suppose she'll be resuming her duties up at the manor for a few days yet."

"I don't think she'll be resuming them at all," said Carrie. "Lucy hated her."

"She didn't give me that impression," said Agatha.

"Well, she did. She once told Harriet that Mrs. Jackson was always poking her nose into things and reading letters. Are you sure you want Mrs. Jackson?"

"I'll see. Is there anyone else?" asked

Agatha, but more as a matter of form because she didn't want anyone else. Mrs. Jackson would surely be the best source of gossip.

"No one who's free. Mrs. Crite does for the vicar and she always says that's enough for her. The summer people usually fend for themselves," said Polly. "Now I do all my own housework. I don't hold a woman paying someone to do what they ought to be doing themselves."

"Good for you," commented Agatha sweetly. "But it's so important not to inflict one's prejudices on anyone else, don't you think? I must be going. Charles, let's . . . Charles?"

She swung round. Charles had moved a little away and was whispering to Carrie, who was blushing and giggling.

"What were you up to?" asked Agatha angrily as she and Charles walked on.

"Just chatting. Jealous, Aggie?"

"Of course not. Don't be silly."

Carrie had been wearing tight jeans and high-heeled boots. She had good legs. And so have I, thought Agatha, when I'm not wearing these clumpy flat shoes. They turned into the other lane and so to the garage. A man in overalls was peering at the engine of a car.

"Mrs. Jackson live near here?" asked Charles.

The man straightened up. "Take that little path at the side there. You can see the chimbleys behind the trees."

They followed his directions and arrived at a seedy-looking cottage thatched in Norfolk reed. It needed rethatching, the thatch being dusty and broken. The front garden was a mess of weeds with various discarded children's toys scattered around.

Agatha rang the bell. "I didn't hear it ring," said Charles. "Probably broken." He knocked at the door. The door was opened by Barry Jones, the gardener.

"What are you doing here?" asked Agatha.

"Came home to Mum's for a bite to eat."

"Mum? But you're a Jones."

"Mum's first husband was a Jones."

"Can we talk to her?" asked Charles.

"Okay, but she's a bit tired. Police here all morning."

They walked into a stone-flagged kitchen, which out-messed Framp's. Dishes were piled in the sink, the old fuel-burning stove was thick with grease and piled with dirty pots.

Betty Jackson was sitting at the kitchen table, mopping up egg with a slice of bread. It seems to be all-day breakfast around here,

113

thought Agatha, thinking of Framp.

"What is it?" she asked dully.

"I'm looking for a cleaner," said Agatha brightly. "What a picturesque cottage you have. I do love these old cottages."

"All right for folks like you," said Mrs. Jackson sourly. "I would like one of them new council ones they'd got over at Purlett End Village. But would they give me one? Naw!"

Charles slid into the chair next to her. "Police been giving you a bad time?"

"Yerse. Them and their tomfool questions. I told them, I left at five and that's that."

"Who would do such a thing?" Charles took one of Mrs. Jackson's red and swollen hands and gave it a squeeze.

"I don't know," said the cleaner, but in a much softer voice. Agatha, seeing that no one was going to ask her to sit down, jerked out a chair.

"Weren't relations between Tolly and Lucy a bit strained?" Charles's voice was soft and coaxing.

"Oh, no." She shook her head. "Devoted couple, they was."

"You see, Lucy Trumpington-James did tell Mrs. Raisin here that she thought her husband was being unfaithful to her."

Mrs. Jackson's heavy face registered shock and she gave her dentures an angry click. "That's rubbish. I tell you what it was; Lucy got fits of jealousy, she was that mad about him, but they always made up. Fact is, she was laughing about it with him before she left for London. She says to him, she says, 'I told that old trout who thinks she's a detective that you was having it off with Rosie.' And they both had a laugh about that."

Agatha coloured angrily. Then she heard Charles say, "About the cleaning?"

"It's seven pounds an hour."

Agatha was about to yell that she was not going to pay London rates to a bad-tempered slut when Charles surprised her by leaping to his feet and putting his arms round her. "Shut up," he whispered. Then he turned to Mrs. Jackson. "Why not start tomorrow? At ten, say. Nothing like work to keep your mind off things."

"Right you are, sir."

Charles smiled and propelled the raging Agatha out of the cottage. Agatha held her temper until they were out of earshot and then she confronted him with "How could you? I don't want that old bitch around my cottage."

"Calm down. Be nice to her and you might get the truth out of her. You only came here to employ her to get gossip." He took her shoulders and gave her a little shake. "Just *think*, woman! Did Lucy give you the impression of a wildly jealous wife?"

"Well, no," said Agatha. "Not in the slightest. She looks like some bimbo who married for money and despises her husband."

"So, isn't that interesting? And why would the horrible Mrs. Jackson lie about it? She doesn't strike me as the staunch and loyal servant type."

Agatha's anger ebbed away as she considered this. "No," she said slowly. "So why would she say such a thing? Of course she could simply have been out to humiliate me out of sheer nastiness."

"Could be. Let's go and get a car and drive somewhere for a drink. Rosie's pub will be full of reporters."

As they approached the village green, the pub door opened and several pressmen came out dragging one of their fellows. Their faces were boozy and flushed. Their intention appeared to be to dump a weedy colleague in the duck pond. Rosie appeared in the pub doorway and called to them to stop. They all crowded back into the pub except the weedy one, who set off away from the pub at a jogtrot, occasionally looking back over his shoulder like some weak animal rejected by the herd.

"I thought they would all have been out at the manor," said Charles.

"No," replied Agatha, wise in the ways of the press. "They'll have been out there already. Hand will have told them that he will say nothing until a press conference at, say, about four o'clock."

"But you would think they'd all be knocking on doors in the village for background."

"They'll get around to it. As long as there's a pub, they'll move in a bunch. They feel they're safe just so long as they all keep together. That way they can drink as much as they want and not run the fear of being scooped."

"So what about the one that's run off?"

"They obviously don't rate him highly. It's not always like this. But if one of them's a bully, he becomes the leader of the pack and they all stick together, swearing to share any morsels of information, and yet each one is privately determined to scoop the others at the first opportunity."

"Excuse me."

A voice behind them made them jump. They swung round. The weedy reporter had come back. "I'm Gerry Philpot of *The Radical Voice*," he said. The paper he represented claimed to have unbiased views, the sort of paper which reported on the "warring factions" in Bosnia to avoid pointing out the obvious truth, that the Serbs were murdering everyone. It was a sitting-on-the-fence and pontificating sort of newspaper which paid the lowest wages, hence Gerry Philpot, a youngish man with weak eyes, receding hair, a pea-green jacket, checked shirt, shabby corduroys and red tie. "Have you heard about the murder?"

"Yes," said Agatha before Charles could say anything. "We were the last people to see Tolly Trumpington-James alive."

"Really!" His eyes lit up. He pulled out a notebook. "If I can just get your name?"

"Mrs. Agatha Raisin."

"Age?"

"Forty-five," lied Agatha, ignoring Charles's snort of laughter.

"And you, sir?"

"This is Sir Charles Fraith," said Agatha quickly, knowing that Charles would not use his title and Agatha was out to impress.

"Age?"

"Thirty-two," said Charles maliciously. He was, in fact, in his forties.

"And you have lived here, how long?"

"Only a few days," said Agatha. "Sir Charles is my house guest."

"What brought you to Fryfam?"

"Just a whim. I'd never been to Norfolk before. I've only been here a short while. As a matter of fact, when it to comes to crime — "

But the reporter interrupted her impatiently. "So tell me how Mr. Trumpington-James seemed to you when you saw him."

"Bit fussed over the robbery of his Stubbs. Police all over the place. I'd had tea with himself and his wife two days before."

"And how did they seem? A happy couple?"

Agatha was not prepared to tell the press about Lucy's suspicions and so she said, "I couldn't really judge. Their cleaner, a Mrs. Jackson, lives behind the garage. She could tell you more than I could."

Gerry cast a longing look towards the pub. His faithless photographer was in there. He was wondering if he could winkle him out without alerting the others. But for the moment he persevered, asking Agatha what the manor looked like inside, had Tolly been very rich and so on. Then he said, "I'll just go and see this Mrs. Jackson. Where do you both live when you're not in Fryfam?"

They gave their home addresses. As he was about to leave, Agatha said, "Oh, have you heard about the fairies?"

Gerry, who had been closing his notebook, opened it again and stared at her. "Fairies?"

Agatha could hear Polly's voice asking her not to say anything, but her desire to shine was greater than any loyalty to the women of Fryfam. She told Gerry about the mysterious lights and the petty thefts, ending up in the grand theft of the Stubbs. When she had finally finished, Gerry's face was red with excitement. "Where do you live? I mean, in Fryfam?"

"Lavender Cottage, over there in Pucks Lane."

"I'll call on you with a photographer if I may."

"We're going out," said Charles.

"But if you can make it quick," put in Agatha. If she got her picture in the newspaper, then James, wherever he was, might see it.

"So you're thirty-two," jeered Agatha as she and Charles walked off.

"Well, if you're forty-five, sweetie, I'm definitely thirty-two."

Agatha could feel herself aging by the minute as they walked home, like She when the Eternal Flame didn't work anymore. She was grumpy and guilty because she had told the reporter about the fairies.

***

Gerry sidled into the pub. The reporters and photographers were all swapping tall tales of their own adventures, and in the middle of the noisiest group was his photographer, Jimmy Henshaw. He was just wondering how to get Jimmy away from the group when the pub door opened and a television crew entered. The newspaper reporters, who all affected to despise television and yet were secretly longing to see their faces on the screen, surged forward to surround the newcomers. Gerry caught Jimmy by the arm and whispered, "I've got a great story. Meet me outside."

Gerry went outside again and chewed his thumb nervously, watching the pub door. Just when he thought Jimmy was never going to emerge, the photographer appeared, lugging his camera case.

"This had better be good," he said sulkily. Rapidly Gerry outlined the story of the fairies.

"Great," said Jimmy. "Let's go and see these people."

Agatha had not expected them so soon and had therefore had not had time to apply that thick layer of make-up, so necessary when being photographed by the press if one did not want to appear ten years older. And she was still wearing her flat shoes. But she led them down the garden and pointed to the place where she had seen the mysterious lights.

"Don't point," said the cameraman sharply. "Looks so damn amateur when people point. Just stand there, Agatha, by that tree, next to Charlie. No, don't smile."

When they had left, Agatha groaned, "Why did I ever tell that reporter about the fairies?"

"Wanted glory?" suggested Charles. "Come on, let's get out of this village and find somewhere to eat."

At last, seated over a late lunch at a road-side pub on the way to Norwich, Charles said, "What I'm wondering about is this. You seem eager to believe that Rosie is innocent, that Lucy made up all that about Tolly having an affair with her. What if it was all true? What if Tolly planned to run away with Rosie? Lucy somehow nips back from London, slits Tolly's throat, and rushes back."

"I've a feeling it will be proved she was in London all the time," said Agatha. "Now if it were in a book, she would turn out to be a motorcycle fiend or had a friend with a private helicopter. Anyway, all she really wanted from Tolly was Tolly's money, I'm sure of that. If he did run away with Rosie, then all she had to do was divorce him and live happily ever after off the alimony."

"But why would anyone else want to kill him?"

"Maybe the hunt got tired of him."

"Joke. But the hunt could be a good start. We'll find out the name of the master and go and see him."

"How will we do that?"

"Anyone will tell us. Framp will tell us. Have you got a mobile phone?"

"Yes." Agatha produced one from her handbag. Charles phoned directory in-quiries and got the number of the Fryfam police station. He then phoned Framp and asked for the name of the master.

Framp was obviously asking why he wanted to know, for Agatha heard Charles say that he might be staying on longer than expected and would like a bit of hunting. Then Charles made writing motions and Agatha produced a pen and small notebook from her bag. Charles wrote busily, then thanked Framp and rang off.

"Here we are. Captain Tommy Findlay, The Beeches, Breakham, and Breakham is that village we drove through, not far from

Fryfam. Drink up your coffee and let's go see him."

Agatha was aware, as Charles drove her away from the pub, of the mobile phone resting in her handbag. She had a sudden longing to telephone Mrs. Bloxby, but Charles would listen and so she couldn't talk about James. She felt a wave of homesickness, a longing for her own home. She was glad she had brought her cats and wished she had thought to buy them a little treat, like fresh fish.

She worried about that reporter, Gerry. He had predictably said he didn't like cats. Men usually said they didn't like cats but then went on to brag about their own cat, which was somehow an exception to the rule.

Maybe the newspaper wouldn't publish his story. Maybe he was such a failure that they would take their news from one of the agencies and ignore his.

"Here we are," said Charles, turning up a lane bordered by high hedges. He drove past a farm, through a farmyard, over a cattle grid and so to a square eighteenth-century house.

"Maybe we should have phoned first," said Agatha.

She started to get out of the car and then retreated back inside and slammed the door as three dogs, one Jack Russell, one Irish setter, and one Border collie, rushed barking towards them.

But Charles was out of the car and patting the dogs and talking to them. "Come on, Aggie," he shouted. "They won't eat you."

Agatha got out and hurried up to Charles as the dogs sniffed about her. Charles rang the bell. I hope no one's at home, thought Agatha, pushing away the collie, which had thrust its nose up her skirt. The door was opened by a small faded woman in an apron. "Mrs. Findlay?" said Charles. "Is the captain at home?"

She peered myopically at him. "If you're collecting for something or selling something, it's not a good time."

"Would you tell him Sir Charles Fraith wants to speak to him about getting some hunting?"

"Of course, Sir Charles. Come in. I don't see very well without my glasses." Charles walked in and Mrs. Findlay shut the door in Agatha's face. Agatha was just planning to kick the door when it opened again and Charles, with a broad grin on his face, said, "Come along."

"Stupid woman," grumbled Agatha.

"Have I become invisible or something?"

"She doesn't see very well."

He led her into a dark hall where a flustered Mrs. Findlay was waiting. "My husband's in the study."

Captain Findlay was a very tall man. Agatha guessed he might be in his seventies but he looked fit, with a lean brown face, bright brown eyes and thick grey hair.

The study was as dark as the hall and smelt strongly of wood-smoke and damp dog. There were oil paintings of hunts on the wall, rather dingy and, even to Agatha's inexpert eye, badly executed.

"Sit down," said the captain. "Get them some tea, Lizzie. Hop to it!"

Agatha almost expected the meek and myopic Mrs. Findlay to drop a curtsy before she left the room.

"Now, to what do I owe this visit?" asked the captain.

"We were interested in finding out your views on Tolly Trumpington-James," said Charles.

"Why?"

"Well, he's been murdered, for a start."

"What's it to you?"

"We both knew Tolly and Lucy — "

"Then you'll know more about them than me."

126

"But you hunted with Tolly," Charles lied. "Surely you can tell a lot about a man's character on the hunting field."

"That's true." The captain, who had been standing in front of a small smouldering fire, suddenly sat down in a battered armchair. "He was a dreadful rider. Had an old hunter like an animated sofa but he still seemed to fall off it every now and then. Lot of time wasted picking him up. But he was generous at fund-raising dinners, that sort of thing. Pathetically anxious to join in. I admired him in a way. It was no wonder he was a successful businessman, the way he stuck to hunting and kept turning up for the meets although he must have been black and blue. Wife's pretty, but a bit sulky. She turned up at various hunt dinners and glared around, smoked and drank too much. Made no effort to fit in."

"Why should she?" asked Agatha crossly. "It was Tolly who wanted to belong."

"It's a wife's job to support her husband," said the captain sharply. "I remember when Lizzie told me she'd got a job as a secretary in Norwich. I soon put a stop to that."

Agatha sighed and relapsed into silence, wondering if there might not be another murder soon.

"Mark my words," the captain went on.

"The wife did it."

"But she was in London," said Charles gently.

"Probably got friends to lie for her. Who else would want to kill Tolly?" His eyes sharpened, "I really don't see what all this has to do with you."

Charles flashed a look at Agatha to warn her not to launch into a description of their detecting abilities, but Agatha appeared sunk in gloom. "We just wanted to do what we could to help Lucy," said Charles.

A slight frost entered the captain's fine eyes. "I can't help you any further. Do you hunt?"

"No," said Charles.

The frost was now pure ice. "Thought not, even though you used it as an excuse to lie your way in here." He got to his feet. "I'll see you out."

They nearly collided in the doorway with Mrs. Findlay, who was staggering under the weight of a laden tea-tray.

"What are you bringing tea for, you silly woman?" barked the captain.

"You asked for tea, dear."

"They haven't got time. They're just going."

"If I were married to someone like that,

I'd shoot myself," said Agatha when they were in the car.

"You nearly were."

"What are you talking about?"

"James Lacey."

"What! James would never behave like that."

"Suit yourself. I think he would, given time and aging."

"Let's talk about this case," said Agatha testily. "I don't think we really got anything there we didn't know."

"Hunts are expensive and Tolly was anxious to ingratiate himself. It still points to Lucy. What if she saw all the money leaching away and knew she wasn't going to end up with much even if she found grounds to divorce him. Maybe she thieved the Stubbs first. Maybe she resented the money he paid for it and did it for revenge and then killed him in a rage."

"She's got that alibi, and besides, cutting a man's throat isn't a female crime."

"How could anyone creep up behind a man on a landing and slit his throat?"

"We don't know the details," said Agatha. "He might have been in bed, asleep, when his throat was slit, and then staggered out to the landing."

"But wouldn't Mrs. Jackson be talking

about there being blood everywhere?"

"Huh! Hardly one of the world's talkers is our Mrs. Jackson."

"We've got visitors," said Charles as they drove up to Lavender Cottage.

"Les girls." Agatha saw Polly, Carrie and Harriet turning round at the sound of the car.

"Let's see if there's any more gossip," said Charles.

The three greeted them with cries of "Isn't it awful? Have the police been to see you again? Lucy's back from London but she's with the police."

Agatha unlocked the door and shepherded them all through to the kitchen. "I think we could all do with a drink," she said. "Charles, could you attend to them?"

Charles took their orders and vanished towards the sitting-room to collect the drinks. Three curious pairs of eyes followed his well-tailored back. "So nice to have a man friend around at a time like this," said Carrie. "Are you engaged?"

Before Agatha could reply, Polly said, "Of course they're not."

"Why do you say that?" demanded Agatha.

"Age difference," remarked Polly bluntly.

"Never mind my private life," said Agatha

crossly. "What's the latest about the murder?"

"Paul Redfern, the gamekeeper, says that Tolly often confided in him and Tolly had said only the other week that he was tired of his wife complaining about the country and he had told her if she liked London so much she could go back and live there, but he wouldn't support her, she'd have to get a job," said Harriet.

"But she has an alibi," said Agatha, wondering how many times she was going to say that. "She has, hasn't she?"

"Evidently so. Oh, thanks," said Harriet, taking a glass of gin and tonic from Charles. "One of the policemen told Paul, who told Sarah at the dried-flower shop, who told me that she says she was staying with a friend, Melissa Carson in South Ken, near the tube, something mansions or other, and they had gone out for dinner at a restaurant in the Brompton Road and then had an early night, so she couldn't have got to Norfolk. Such a pity when she's such an obvious suspect. That awful man, Hand, has been poking about and making everyone in the village feel guilty."

"I wonder if either of them was having an affair," mused Agatha.

"I shouldn't think so," said Polly. "You

can't keep anything quiet around here."

"But they may not have been carrying on with anyone in the village," said Agatha. "I mean, Tolly might have been having an affair with one of the wives of the huntsmen."

"But that would mean the murderer would have to be Lucy," protested Carrie.

"Not necessary. It could mean the cuckolded huntsman," said Charles.

"I wish it were all over," sighed Harriet. "First those dancing lights, and now this. At least the village has stayed solid."

"About what?" asked Agatha.

"The lights, of course. We don't want everyone saying we're some yokel nuts who believe in fairies."

Charles looked quizzically at Agatha, who said rapidly, "I think someone's bound to have said something. I mean, look at all the gossip that came out of the gamekeeper. Where does he live?"

"He's got a cottage on the estate. He's wondering what's going to happen to him now."

There was a ring at the doorbell. "I'll get it," said Charles. He returned and said to Agatha, "It's Hand and his sidekick. I've put them in the sitting-room."

Agatha suppressed a groan. The three woman rose rapidly to their feet. "We'd best be going. We've had enough of the police," said Polly.

Reluctantly, Agatha went through to the sitting-room. With a sinking heart, she noticed Hand was clutching her manuscript.

"Just a few more questions, Mrs. Raisin. Do you not think it a remarkable coincidence that the owner of the manor in your book should have his throat cut and that Mr. Trumpington-James should be murdered in the same way?"

"Remarkable," said Agatha wearily.

"Where were you on the night of the murder?"

"I went to the pub with Charles and we came back here."

"I suppose you will vouch for him and he will vouch for you?"

"Yes, but look here. Neither of us knew the Trumpington-Jameses before we came here. What motive would we have?"

"Well, let's take you, for instance. We've been checking up on you. You seem to have been involved in a lot of murders and you are not shy of publicity. Let's say, you know the value of publicity. You ran a public relations firm before you took early retirement."

"So where's this leading?" asked Agatha, wondering where Charles was and why he wasn't in the sitting-room, supporting her.

"The point is this." Hand held up the manuscript. "Now this is not well-written. But some publisher might offer a hefty sum for it because of the tie-in with the murder."

"You potty man," said Agatha furiously. "Are you trying to say that I would come all the way to Norfolk to bump someone off just to get a book sold?"

"We are just examining all the angles."

"Examine this! I do not know how to operate Tolly's burglar alarm, and whoever did must have murdered him, which leaves only Mrs. Jackson or Lucy."

Hand looked at her with mournful eyes. "If only it were as simple as that. Not only did Mrs. Jackson know the code, but the gamekeeper, the gardener and most of the hunt."

"What?"

"Mr. Trumpington-Jones, after he had the burglar-alarm system installed, kept forgetting the code. He got drunk at a hunt dinner and kept telling everyone who would listen to write it down for him so they could remind him."

"So what was the point of having a burglar-alarm system installed in the first place?"

"Oh, he evidently told his wife that they

were all decent chaps around here. It was to protect him from city thieves, not local people."

"I can't tell you anything further," said Agatha. "Like I said, that death in my book and the death of Tolly is sheer coincidence. How on earth could I think that anyone in this day and age would use a cutthroat razor?" She looked sharply at Hand. "It was his own razor, wasn't it?"

"I see no harm in telling you. No, it wasn't his own razor."

"Oh, then, it should be easy to trace the owner. I read a Dorothy Sayers's detective story where — "

"Spare us," said Hand nastily. "You can still buy cutthroat razors at boot sales and in some antique shops."

"It still strikes me as a daft idea. Why not just club him or poison him?"

"This way would be fast and deadly and quiet," said Hand.

Where was Charles? "Don't you want to question Sir Charles further?" asked Agatha.

"Not at the moment." Hand rose to his feet.

"May I have my manuscript back?"

"We'll keep it for the moment. I assume you have a copy of this on your computer?"

"Yes, but — "

"So you won't be needing this. We'll be in touch."

Charles was lurking in the hall when Agatha let the police out.

She was about to berate him for having left her alone with the police when the phone rang. She picked up the receiver. It was Mrs. Bloxby. "I heard about the murder on television," said the vicar's wife. "Are you all right?"

"Yes, I'm fine. Charles is here, although," added Agatha waspishly, "he's not much help."

Charles grinned and strolled off into the kitchen.

"So you'll be staying on for a bit?"

"I feel I have to. To see if I can solve the murder."

"Why? You're not connected to anyone there."

"The thing is this: I thought I'd try my hand at writing a detective story. This was before the murder."

"But I don't see — "

"Listen!" said Agatha. "I called the damned thing *Death at the Manor* and in the book the owner of the manor gets his throat cut with an open razor and bingo, the owner here goes and gets his throat cut with an open razor. And what's worse, I based the characters on those of Tolly Trumpington-James and his wife, so you see . . . Are you *laughing?*" she demanded angrily as a stifled snort sounded down the phone.

Another snort and then chuckles. "I'd better go," said Agatha furiously.

"No, wait!" Mrs. Bloxby recovered herself. "I've a bit of news."

"What?" asked Agatha sulkily.

"I was passing James's cottage the other day and that girl he let use it was packing stuff into a car. She said she'd had a postcard from James, and James is expected back next week."

Agatha felt as if she had been punched in the stomach.

Then she said slowly, "I'll stay on for a bit, you know. The police are still asking me questions."

"I'm sure they are," said Mr. Bloxby with a giggle.

"Goodbye. I've got to go." Agatha slammed down the phone and marched into the kitchen. "You'll never believe it," she stormed at Charles. "I told Mrs. Bloxby about the mess I'd got into because I wrote that detective story and she *laughed.*"

"Think of it, Aggie," said Charles. "It's such a sort of Agatha Raisin thing to have done."

"I don't see . . . Oh, I suppose it is funny in way." They both began to laugh helplessly. At last Agatha recovered and wiped her eyes. "What a lot of ghouls we are. Poor Tolly. We shouldn't laugh. What are we to do now?"

"I think we should relax for what's left of the day and tackle Mrs. Jackson in the morning."

The vicar of Carsely, Alf Bloxby, came into the room just as his wife was replacing the receiver. "What was so funny?" he asked.

"That was Agatha Raisin." She told him about the coincidence of Agatha's story and the murder. "I shouldn't have laughed," she said contritely. "I mean, it's not at all funny. That poor man. Why did I laugh, Alf?"

He sighed. "We're like the police and the press, we deal with so many sad cases that sometimes inappropriate laughter is our way of coping with things. Shouldn't you be on your way to see Mrs. Marble?"

"Yes, I'm just going." Alf was right, thought Mrs. Bloxby, as she walked through the village. Take Mrs. Marble, for instance. The poor woman was dying of cancer. But she was querulous, bitter and demanding. She had made out a new will, cutting out her daughter and grandchildren and leaving all her money to a cat's home. Mrs. Bloxby had tried in vain to get her to make a more reasonable will. Occasional jokes with her husband about the terrible Mrs. Marble enabled her to go on calling on her, and doing what she could to help. Humour was a necessary weapon against the pains and tribulations of life.

FIVE

†

Agatha tossed and turned all night, wondering what to do. Part of her longed to rush back to Carsely and get her cottage ready, to visit the beautician, the hairdresser, the dress shops, to prepare for James's arrival. The sensible part of her mind told her that it would be a waste of time. She and James would never be friends again.

Around dawn, she suddenly fell into a heavy sleep and did not wake until ten in the morning. She got out of bed, amazed that the police had not been hammering on the door. She put on a dressing-gown and trailed down to the kitchen.

Charles was sitting at the kitchen table, newspapers spread out in front of him.

"Anything interesting?" asked Agatha.

"Oh, yes. *The Radical Voice*. Front page. 'The Fairies of Fryfam.'"

"God. They'll lynch me in this village. I

would have thought the other papers would have been beating on the door."

"They were. You were fast asleep. I expected the onslaught, so I drove both our cars at dawn out of the village and hid them in a side road and didn't answer the door. They assumed we had both fled."

"Should I read it?"

"Gerry's precious prose? No, better not."

"Let me see it." Agatha sat down opposite him and seized *The Radical Voice*. The first awful sight that met her eyes was a coloured photograph of herself and Charles. Charles looked dapper and amused. But she! The camera had cruelly accentuated every line on her face. "Is that grey hairs?" she asked, peering closely at the photograph.

"You've got a few grey roots," said Charles.

Agatha read the article with growing dismay. It would be clear to everyone in the village that Agatha Raisin had babbled about the fairies, and at great length. Now she definitely had a good excuse to go home.

"They'll lynch me," she said. "I was going back to Carsely anyway. Better go home today."

"James home?"

Agatha blushed angrily. His eyes searched her face. "But he's coming home. Last night after that phone call from Mrs. Bloxby, you were elated one minute and fidgety and miserable the next. We've talked about this before. A friend of mind went to a very good therapist in Harley Street for your problem."

"I don't have a problem."

"Oh, yes, you do. You are a grown woman who is obsessing over a cold man. Before you go back to Carsely, which you should not do until we discover a bit more about this murder, you should go to this therapist first. Just think how free you would feel if you didn't care, Agatha. Think of facing James again and *not caring*. How long is it since you had any *fun* with James? No, don't yell at me off the top of your head. Think!"

Agatha said, "I don't like to be bullied."

"You don't like a sensible suggestion either. Promise me you'll at least try this therapist."

"Anything to shut you up. Where's Mrs. Jackson?"

"I called her at her cottage and told her not to come until tomorrow."

"We can't hide in here all day."

"No, we'll walk a back route to the cars, take yours and go to Norwich, where you will get your hair done."

"I s'pose," grumbled Agatha. "I'd better have some breakfast."

"By which you mean two cups of coffee and three cigarettes. The coffee's ready in the pot and your cigarettes are on the table."

"What on earth is Hand going to say about these fairies? He'll say I've been holding out on him."

"He'll know about the lights. I can't see Tolly holding back that bit of information when Hand was investigating the theft of the Stubbs."

The day was quiet and misty, a grey, dreamy landscape. They set out looking to right and left to make sure no reporter was lurking in the bushes. Charles had warned her to wear her wellingtons and carry her shoes, for the way he took her led over a stile at the end of Pucks Lane and across a field of stubble.

They climbed over another stile and into a lane to where he had parked the cars at the end of it. Agatha removed her muddy boots and put on her shoes. She drove off slowly through the mist and onto the main road. "We can't hide out forever," she said.

"Give it another day and you won't be the only one to have talked about fairies. In fact, I'll bet you if we watch the news when we get back, some of them will be standing in front of a camera talking happily about the little people. It always amazes me how people will refuse to talk to newspaper reporters and yet welcome a television crew into their homes."

"We'll have lunch in Norwich first," said Agatha, "and then I'll leave you to entertain yourself while I find a hairdresser."

Charles waited by Agatha's car in a parking lot in Norwich. They had arranged to meet at five o'clock. The mist had lifted and a late sun was shining down. Then he saw Agatha coming towards him and smiled. Her thick hair was once more a glossy brown. Her face had been skillfully made up. She was wearing a new jacket and skirt in a soft heathery tweed. Her excellent legs were encased in fine tights, ending in a new pair of court shoes. Agatha, reflected Charles, would never be a beauty, but she carried with her a strong aura of sexual magnetism of which she was entirely unaware.

"You clean up a treat," he said. "Let's see if we can get back in time for the six-o'clock news."

"Do I have to struggle across that muddy field again?"

"No, deadline time's over for the newspapers and they'll all be in the pub. Drop me at my car and then we'll both drive home."

Agatha was dying to phone Mrs. Bloxby again, to ask more about James's return. But the cottage was small and Charles would hear her and Charles would start nagging her about that therapist again.

Agatha had a leisurely bath that evening, creamed her face, put on her night-dress and went into her bedroom. Charles was lying on her bed with his hands clasped behind his head.

"What are you doing there?" demanded Agatha.

"I thought we might . . ."

"No. Absolutely not."

"Not even a cuddle?"

"No."

He sighed and swung his legs out of bed and then made for the door. "Saving yourself for James?" he jeered.

"Just go away!" shouted Agatha and slammed the door behind him.

She had slept with Charles before, only to find out that he had gone off romancing some other female the day after. Agatha got into bed and lay staring at the ceiling. To take her mind off the imminent return of James, she began to turn what she knew about Tolly's murder over in her mind, and the more she thought about it, the stranger it seemed. She began to think that the theft of the Stubbs might not have anything to do with the murder. So concentrate on the murder alone. Lucy was the only suspect. Agatha was sure that Lucy had been telling the truth when she had suspected Tolly was having an affair. Based on what? Rose perfume and the fact that Tolly had washed the sheets. But Rosie Wilder, Agatha was sure, had been telling the truth. But surely rose perfume could be used by anyone.

The best thing would be to wait until the fuss died down and then try to see Lucy. Charles had been right about one thing — the evening television news had featured many of the locals, including Harriet, talking about the fairies.

By the next day, Agatha began to wonder if the fuss would ever die down. And for the following week, the village of Fryfam was under a sort of siege. "You did this," Polly shouted at Agatha when she met her crossing the village green. Because of the fairies, not only tourists but weirdos had descended on the village. And then came the New Age travellers, that scourge of the countryside, with their savage dogs and dirty children, their broken-down trailers and trucks camped on the village green. They were finally routed by the police and left in a haze of filthy exhaust, leaving the village green like a tip and not a duck left on the pond because they had eaten the lot.

So it was with something like surprise that Agatha opened the door one morning to Harriet and Polly.

"Can I help you?" she asked nervously.

"Yes, you can," said Polly. "We are all getting together to clean up the village green." She handed Agatha a roll of garbage bags.

Glad to be no longer ostracized, Agatha agreed. She called to Charles to come and help but he appeared to have become suddenly deaf because there was no reply to her calls. She went off with Harriet and Polly. "I'm sorry about that fairy business," said Agatha. "It just slipped out."

"Well, you're no longer the culprit, everyone in the village seems to have spouted off about fairies to the television cameras," said Polly, sour because no one had asked her about them. "Has Mrs. Jackson been cleaning for you?"

"Not yet," said Agatha. "She's been due to call several times but she always says she's poorly. Has anyone seen Lucy?"

They both shook their heads. "We hear she's up at the manor and the lawyers have called," said Polly, "and the police are still there the whole time."

"Oh, dear," murmured Agatha as they came upon the full horror of the village green.

"That's not all," said Harriet with gloomy relish. "Those pesky travellers were using the pond as a toilet, so we're getting someone down from the Department of the Environment to advise us how best to purify the water."

Several other villagers were working alongside them. "This is all the fault of that Lucy Trumpington-James," complained a stout countrywoman to Agatha. Agatha straightened up from her rubbish collection. "How's that?" she asked.

"If she hadn't have murdered him, then these dirty folks wouldn't have come here."

"But she was in London."

"So they say, but don't you believe it."

"Was Tolly Trumpington-James having an affair with anyone?" asked Agatha.

"Why shouldn't he?" demanded the woman, her red hands on her broad hips. "Wasn't much fun being married to her."

"So who was he having an affair with?" said Agatha eagerly.

"I never said nothing," retorted the woman angrily and walked quickly away to another part of the green.

I must find out more about this, thought Agatha. She called to Polly and Harriet, who had been joined by Carrie, "When you're ready for a break, we can go back to my place for coffee."

"Right," said Harriet. "We'll let you know."

Agatha was just wondering if she would ever walk straight again when Harriet called, "Wouldn't mind that coffee now."

Agatha straightened up with a groan. Her back was aching. Her fingers were numb because the day was icy cold.

When they were all seated around the kitchen table — still no sign of Charles — Agatha said, "A woman on the green told me Tolly was having an affair."

"Who would that be?" wondered Harriet. "I mean, who told you that?"

"Big, broad woman, rosy cheeks, frizzy grey hair."

"Oh, that would be Daisy Brean. I wonder what she was on about. I never heard anything about Tolly having an affair. I mean, who would want Tolly?"

"We could ask about," suggested Agatha. "I mean, if she knows something, maybe someone else does. And that would mean there might be some angry husband who wanted rid of Tolly."

"I saw Charles the other day," said Carrie, "and he took me for a drink. He said you were thinking of leaving soon but that he might stay on."

Agatha realized that she had been able to put James out of her mind for over a week.

They had played endless games of Scrabble, gone to the cinema in Norwich, gone shopping and had kept away from the villagers as much as possible. Charles had said it was best to keep clear until the fuss died down and the press moved on to juicier stories. So when had he met Carrie? Then she remembered; she had decided to wash and set her hair and he had said he would go out for a walk. Carrie was slim and attractive. Damn Charles, and thank God she hadn't gone to bed with him. She was now determined to stay on longer. If Fryfam could take her mind off James, then it was worth hanging on for a bit. Charles's suggestion that she see a therapist still rankled.

"I'll be here for a bit," said Agatha. "By the way, I like that rose scent that Rosie Wilden uses. Is it a commercial one?"

"No, she makes it."

"Does she sell any?"

"I think she'll give you some if you ask her. She says it's from an old recipe," said Carrie. "I suppose I'd better be going."

150

The others rose as well. As Agatha saw them out, Charles was just returning.

"What now?" she asked.

"Eat something and then we'll go out to the manor to present our condolences to Lucy."

"I'm tired of thinking about meals," said Agatha crossly.

"Doesn't seem to trouble you much. Just bung it in the microwave. Let me see what we've got. I'll make something. Let's see. Eggs, bacon, sausage. That'll do. A nice fry-up."

"I needn't worry about my weight," said Agatha. "I must have lost pounds picking up that garbage."

"Sit there while I make with the frying pan."

"Are you usually so domesticated?"

"Only around you. I'm driven into it."

After lunch, they headed out to the manor, Agatha refusing to walk, saying she had endured enough cold air to last her for the rest of the day. There had been a hard frost during the night and patches of it still lay unmelted on the ground.

"If anyone talks to me about global warming, I'll puke," grumbled Agatha. "It was a rotten summer as well."

"The rest of the world was burning up," said Charles. "Here we are. Gates open. No policeman on duty."

They went up the drive. It all seemed very quiet.

Charles rang the doorbell. They waited for what seemed a long time, until Lucy's voice suddenly sounded from the other side of the door. "Who is it?"

"Charles Fraith and Agatha Raisin."

The door opened. "I thought it might be the press," said Lucy. "Come in."

They followed her into the drawing-room. She was wearing a silky trouser suit and was highly made up, as if about to go on television.

"We were very sorry to hear of Tolly's death," said Agatha.

"Were you?" Lucy raised thin eyebrows. "You barely knew him."

There was an awkward silence. Then Agatha said, "Have you any idea who would murder your husband?"

"No," said Lucy, suddenly looking weary.

"But you wanted me to find out if Tolly had been having an affair."

"Did I?"

"Yes," said Agatha crossly. "You thought he was having an affair with Rosie Wilden. Remember? All about the rose perfume in

152

the bedroom and the fact that Tolly had washed the sheets?"

"Oh, that."

There was a silence.

"Well?" prompted Charles.

"Well, what? Oh, I see. Nothing seems to matter much."

"But don't you see," said Agatha eagerly, "if Tolly was having an affair, then the murder might have been committed by a jealous husband."

"Rosie doesn't have a husband."

"It doesn't need to be her. She might give that perfume of hers to people who ask for it."

"Truth to tell, I've been so shattered by this," said Lucy, "I haven't been able to think clearly. You've got an idea there."

"Didn't you say anything to the police about your suspicions?" asked Charles.

"Them! That man, Hand, went on and on as if I'd done it. I had to have all my wits about me sticking to my alibi."

Agatha wanted to ask her why Mrs. Jackson had said that she and Tolly had been laughing about her suspicions and why they had ridiculed her, Agatha. But Lucy might freeze up. And there was still hope of getting gossip out of Mrs. Jackson — that is, if she ever turned up to clean.

"Did Tolly ever seem to favour any woman?"

"Apart from Rosie, no. He would suck up to wives at hunt dos, ones whose husbands he wanted to ingratiate himself with."

"Like who?" asked Charles.

"Oh, like that dreary old bag, Mrs. Findlay."

"Captain Findlay's wife?"

"Yes, her. I call her the battered bride. She always trembles every time her husband looks at her. He probably beats her."

"And the police have no idea where the Stubbs went to?"

"None at all. It'll probably turn up in some mansion in South America."

"I assume you get everything," said Charles.

"Yes."

"Good solicitors?"

"Old-fashioned and solid. Tomley and Barks in Norwich."

"Tomley," said Charles. "There was a Tristan Tomley in my form at Eton and he came from over here."

"Could be," said Lucy indifferently.

"What will you do now?" asked Agatha.

For the first time, Lucy seemed animated. "I'll sell up here and move to London. Thank God this place and the grounds are worth something. Tolly didn't leave much else. That damn hunt must have been bleeding him dry. I never want to see another horse or hound again."

"We'll do all we can to help," said Agatha.

Lucy gave a little shrug. "I don't see what you can do. But thanks anyway. I'm sorry I haven't offered you anything, but I'm a bit busy at the moment, so . . ."

Agatha and Charles rose to their feet. "Find your own way out?" Lucy remained seated.

They said goodbye and walked out to the car.

"What now?" asked Agatha.

"The solicitors in Norwich."

"They won't tell us anything."

"They might — that is, if the Tomley part of the business is the one I went to school with."

The city of Norwich was shrouded in mist, slowly thickening into fog. "Hope it doesn't get worse than this or we'll need to stay the night here," said Charles. "Do you know, the fairies have disappeared. No more petty theft."

"That's true. Do you think someone stole the petty stuff and flashed lights around to make everyone frightened as a blind, when all the time he really meant to steal the Stubbs?"

"Could be. But there's something about the petty thefts which smacks of the work of children. We never saw Mrs. Jackson's children, apart from the gardener."

"And that's a mystery," said Agatha as Charles eased into the car-park. "How on earth did a woman like that manage to get married two times?"

"No accounting for taste." Charles flashed her a wicked look. "Is there, Aggie?"

"Stop calling me Aggie and let's find this solicitor."

The solicitors' offices were in a pleasant old sixteenth-century flint building in a courtyard off Lower Goat Lane. "Let's hope it's the Tomley I knew and that he's here and not in court," said Charles.

He gave his card to a motherly looking receptionist. She smiled at them, told them to wait, and said she would see if Mr. Tomley was available.

They sat down in comfortable leather armchairs in front of a low table covered in glossy magazines.

The receptionist returned, smiled again, and said, "Mr. Tomley is on the phone. Will you wait? He should only be a few moments."

Agatha picked up a magazine about country houses and flicked through it. The offices were very quiet, protected from the sound of traffic by the courtyard outside. Her eyelids began to droop and soon she was fast asleep.

She awoke with a jerk half an hour later. Charles was shaking her by the shoulder. "Come along, Aggie. We're going for a drink. This is Tommers."

Agatha stood up and blinked blearily and focused on a plump, well-tailored man with a red shiny face and thick grey hair. "You should have woken me, Charles," she admonished.

"You haven't missed anything," said Charles cheerfully, "and you look so beautiful when you sleep, snoring gently and with your mouth hanging open."

"And you make noises like a dog hunting rabbits in *your* sleep. Whoop, whoop, shiver, whoop," said Agatha nastily.

Then she blushed as Tristan Tomley surveyed both of them with bright-eyed interest.

"Let's go," said Charles, his good humour unabated. "Where's the pub, Tommers?"

"Round the corner. The Goat and Boots."

As they walked out into the freezing, foggy air, Tommers said, "I doubt if the pair of you will get back tonight. Fog's bad. I feel in my bones it's going to be a bad winter."

The pub was relatively quiet. They took their drinks to a corner table. "Well, Charles," said Tommers, "what's this all about? Or did you come the whole way here to reminisce about our school-days?"

"Not quite. You see, I'm staying with Agg— Agatha in Fryfam."

"Aha. The Trumpington-James murder. Why should you be interested?"

"We like to solve mysteries," said Charles. "Wanted to ask you about the will."

"I don't mind telling you about that. All straightforward. Everything goes to the wife."

Agatha had then what she considered as being a sudden flash of intuition. "Aha," she said, her bearlike eyes boring into the lawyer's. "But what about the *other* will?"

"What other will?"

Agatha leaned forward eagerly. "The one Tolly was threatening to make just before he was killed. The one in which he cut out his wife and left the money to . . . someone else!"

Tommers surveyed her with amusement. "You mean like in books?" He burst out laughing. "Nothing so sinister. Only one will and no threats of cutting the wife out. I say, Charles. Do you remember old Stuffy?"

Agatha relapsed into gloom as the reminiscence went on. What a waste of a journey! What a foggy freezing place to land up in, only to be made to feel ridiculous.

At last, after what seemed an age, Tommers said he had to be getting home. "Would invite you," he said, "but my mother-in-law is in residence and she's a bit crotchety, to say the least."

After he had left, Charles said, "Did you really think there might have been another will?"

"I hoped there might be the threat of one, or even some mysterious woman who got something in the real will. Now I feel stupid."

"I must admit I was hoping for the same thing. So what do you want to do? Shall we find a hotel?"

"Let's at least try to get back. We can always stop somewhere on the way home. In fact, we can at least stop somewhere for dinner. I don't like to leave the cats on their own. I left some hard food for them and they've got plenty of water, but they will worry about me."

"I think Hodge and Boswell keep each other amused, Aggie."

"But the cottage will be cold."

"Then they'll probably end up under your duvet."

Agatha grabbed his arm. "Look!"

"Look at what?"

"Oh, she's gone."

"What are you talking about?"

"It was there at the end of the street, just in front of that shop window," said Agatha. "I thought I saw the captain's wife, Lizzie Findlay."

"Well, what's so exciting about that?"

"She looked different, all smartened up, heels and trouser suit and make-up."

"How could you see anything in this fog?"

"It parted a bit and the shop window's brightly lit. A bus passed and sent the fog swirling. It probably wasn't her. It was someone who looked the way she would look if she were smartened up. I suppose I'm seeing things because I don't want this nasty cold outing to be entirely wasted. And, damn, I am worrying about those cats."

The rush-hour was building up. Charles eased out into a lane of traffic. "Maybe we should stop somewhere for a bite soon," he said, "and then we can have a clearer road."

"Anywhere you like," said Agatha. "And put the heater on. I'm freezing."

As they eased out of Norwich, the commuter traffic grew less, and the surrounding countryside, blacker and foggier. "I need a

160

break," muttered Charles. "There's a lit-up sort of building ahead, I think, but with this fog I don't know if it's a factory or a pub. Ah, a pub."

He turned right into a car-park. He got out of the car and held up one finger. "I think there's a breeze, Aggie. Just like a faint breath of air. Do you know what the forecast is?"

"No."

"Oh, well, let's see what they've got in the way of food."

The pub turned out to have a small dining-room. The food was of the chicken-in-a-basket-, scampi-in-a-basket-type of meal, along with various sandwiches and baked potatoes with different fillings.

They both ordered chicken and chips. The chicken turned out to be hard and dry and coated in orange breadcrumbs, and the chips were of the nasty frozen variety. But food was food. They washed it down with mineral water, Charles saying that he didn't want to be charged with being over the limit, and as he couldn't drink, he didn't see why Agatha should have that pleasure. "Besides," he said, "people who drink on their own are terribly suspect."

They ate in silence. Charles, to Agatha's amazement, paid the bill. Outside, the fog was as bad as ever. "Going to be pretty hopeless getting back," commented Charles as damp fog swirled about them. "We should try to get back to Norwich for the night."

"I'll drive," said Agatha grimly. "My cats."

"Damn your pesky cats," said Charles in a rare fit of bad temper. "You're turning into an old maid."

"I'm turning into a caring human being," snapped Agatha, "which is more than I can say for you."

"Get in the car. I'll do my best."

"Where's that precious wind of yours?" asked Agatha, as she fastened her seat-belt.

"God knows. Well, here we go into the black nothingness of Norfolk."

They made their way along the road at a steady thirty miles an hour.

"Can't you go faster?" complained Agatha.

"No. Shut up."

After several miles, Charles said, "The wind is rising at last, and just for the moment, it's making things worse."

Odd pillars of fog danced in the head-lights in front of his tired eyes, like grey ghosts. He crested the top of a small hill and suddenly they were out into a clear starry night.

"Amazing," muttered Charles, accelerating.

At last they reached Fryfam and turned into Pucks Lane. "A large brandy, I think, is called for," said Charles, parking alongside the hedge. Agatha fished in her handbag for the enormous door key.

She stopped short on the threshold. "Charles," she said, "the door's open. Did we leave it like that?"

"Of course not. Don't go in, Aggie. There may be someone still there. I said don't go — "

But with a cry of "My cats!" Agatha went straight inside.

Then Charles heard a scream of dismay from Agatha and darted in after her. She was standing in the sitting-room. Everything had been turned over. The drawers in the desk were hanging open. "Hodge and Boswell?" asked Agatha through white lips.

"Wait here. I'll look upstairs."

Charles went upstairs and into both bedrooms. Someone had gone through everything.

He came back down. "I'm phoning the police. Where are you going?"

"To look for the cats."

Agatha went into the kitchen. Cupboards

opened, drawers opened. What had they been searching for?

She went down the garden, calling desperately for her cats. But there was no welcome glint of green eyes in the darkness.

Agatha searched and searched, until Charles came up behind her. "The police are here, Aggie. I'm sure the cats are all right. They're great survivors. Come in out of the cold."

"I should never have left them." Agatha began to sob.

"Here, now." He put an arm round her. "Where's my brave Aggie? It's only old Framp. The heavy mob will be along shortly."

He coaxed her into the sitting-room, where Framp was standing in front of the fireplace.

"Just a few preliminary questions," said Framp, opening his notebook.

"Sit down," said Charles, pressing Agatha down onto the sofa. "Wait a moment and I'll answer all your questions. She's in no fit state. I'll get her a brandy." Charles went over to the cupboard where Agatha kept the drinks, pulled out a brandy bottle and poured her a stiff measure. "I don't suppose you drink on duty," he said to Framp.

"It's a cold night, sir, and a beer wouldn't go amiss."

"We haven't got beer. Here, Aggie. You drink that. We've got whisky, gin, vodka, and a bottle of elderberry wine."

"I wouldn't mind a whisky, sir."

"Right you are. Soda?"

"No, just straight."

Charles gave Framp a glass of whisky and poured himself a brandy. "Sit down," he said to Framp. "It's going to be a long night."

After half an hour, Hand and Carey arrived. "You're lucky," said Hand. "They got us when we were out on another case not far away." Framp deftly slid his glass behind the television set.

Charles answered all the questions over again. Again he simply said they had been shopping in Norwich and had been late arriving home because of the fog. No, he didn't know what anyone could possibly be looking for, or who could have got in without forcing the door. Agatha was roused to go upstairs with Carey to see if all her jewellery was still there. She moved like an automaton, fretting all the while about her lost cats. Then she returned to the sitting-room with Carey.

"Nothing missing, sir," said Carey.

"We'll have the fingerprint boys along

soon," said Hand with a sigh. "Now, you," he said to Agatha. "Have you been going in for any detecting?"

Charles threw Agatha a warning look. "No," lied Agatha. "What about my cats?"

"I'm sure they are somewhere about."

But Agatha was sure they were dead. She should never have brought them here. She should never have run away from Carsely. She promised God she would do anything if only those cats came back. A forensic team arrived and dusted the place for finger-prints. Despite her misery about her cats, Agatha could not help comparing Fryfam to Carsely. Had this happened in Carsely, all the villagers would have gathered to offer sympathy and support. But the fairy-believers of Fryfam stayed in their burrows like hobbits.

By three in the morning, police and foren-sics packed up and left. Agatha and Charles sat side by side on the sofa. Agatha shivered. "It's so cold," she said.

"Tell you what," said Charles. "You stay there for a bit and I'll light this fire and get us warm and then I'll light the fires in the rooms."

Agatha watched dully as he put fire-lighters, paper and logs on the fire and sat back on his heels, watching it blaze up. Then he picked up the empty log basket. "I'll go out to the shed and get some more logs. You be all right?"

Agatha nodded. She stared at the dancing flames. I'm a silly woman, she thought. Why didn't I mind my own business? Why did I come to his hell-hole just to destroy my cats? Who cares who killed Tolly?

She heard the kitchen door crash open. She heard Charles come in and then he said gleefully, "Look what I've got, Aggie."

She twisted her head around and then jumped to her feet. For Charles was carrying Hodge and Boswell.

"Oh, thank God," cried Agatha, the tears of relief running down her face. She patted both cats. "Bring them into the kitchen, Charles, and I'll give them something special."

Charles waited in the kitchen, amused, as Agatha proceeded to open a tin of pâté de foie gras and then one of salmon.

"Don't kill them with kindness," he said, and then went back down the garden, whistling, to get the logs.

Agatha was awakened by the ringing of the doorbell downstairs. She looked at her bedside clock and groaned. Eight in the morning! She struggled into her dressing-gown and hurried downstairs and the bell rang and rang. She opened the door to confront the unlovely features of Mrs. Jackson.

"Came to do yer house," said Betty Jackson, pushing past Agatha. Agatha collected her wits. She wanted to tell this woman to get lost, but there was all that fingerprint dust.

"We had a break-in last night," said Agatha, "and the police were here, so there's fingerprint dust everywhere. I must go back to bed. Don't bother about the bedrooms. Just clean downstairs. Oh, and do the windows."

"I don't do windows."

"Do what you can," said Agatha crossly. "And don't bother my cats. In fact, I'll take them with me." She looked at the cleaner curiously. "You don't seem over-surprised."

"It's incomers," said Mrs. Jackson, taking off her coat. "Never had nothing like this afore the incomers came."

And coming from a woman who was married to a jailbird, that was a bit thick, thought Agatha. But she was too weary to argue. She scooped up her cats and went upstairs with them and plunked them on the end of the bed, climbed in herself and drifted back into sleep.

When she awoke again, it was eleven

o'clock. She hurriedly washed and dressed and went downstairs, followed by the cats. She could heard Charles's voice coming from the kitchen and guessed he was talking to Mrs. Jackson. She took a look in the sitting-room. It was polished and gleaming and free of dust and the fireplace had been cleaned out and the fire reset. At least she can clean, thought Agatha.

She went into the kitchen. The conversation stopped abruptly when she opened the kitchen door. Mrs. Jackson was rinsing out a cloth at the sink and Charles had the morning papers spread out in front of him.

"Nearly finished here," said Mrs. Jackson. "Want me to do upstairs?"

"Yes, if you please," said Agatha.

Charles rose. "We're going out, Betty. Just let yourself out and lock the door."

"How can she do that?" asked Agatha. "I've got the key."

"I went down to the estate agent's and got another," said Charles. "I've paid Betty. Come along, Aggie. You can eat later."

"So it's Betty now," said Agatha. "What did you get out of her?"

"Get in the car and I'll tell you."

"Wait a bit. Will the cats be all right?"

"I let them into the garden. They'll be fine."

"What does she do with her children when she starts so early?"

"They get the early school bus. The school supplies free breakfasts to the children of working mothers provided they're poor enough."

"So what did you get out of her?"

Charles pulled into a lay-by and switched off the engine. "It's what I didn't get out of her that fascinated me. She says Lucy was a good employer."

"Was? Isn't she working for her any-more?"

"No, she says that Lucy paid her off and very generously, too. Seems as if our Lucy is going to put the house on the market as soon as she can and says she'll get a commercial firm in to do the whole place over. But you would think that someone like Lucy would want someone in the meantime to wash the dirty dishes and Hoover. Mrs. Jackson doesn't talk much about Tolly but sticks to her story that they were a devoted couple."

"Maybe we're wrong. Maybe they were."

"Come on. You don't believe that."

"No, I suppose not. Where are we going?"

"A little of Betty Jackson goes a long way.

There's something about that woman that makes my flesh creep. I've been thinking about Lizzie Findlay."

"The captain's wife? Because I thought I saw her all glammed up?"

"I suppose it's because I'm restless and can't think of anything else. Remember Lucy said something to the effect that Tolly was crawling to Lizzie."

"Yes, but surely that was only to ingratiate himself with the captain."

"I don't know. Take Lucy, for instance. She must spend a fortune on her appearance and she's as hard as nails. There's downtrodden Lizzie, everything that Lucy is not."

"But she's so dowdy and faded!"

"We don't know how she shapes up if she takes a bit of care with her appearance."

Agatha thought about Lizzie. She had not really noticed her. Myopic, wispy hair, figure hidden in shapeless garments. She shook her head. "Not possible."

"Let's go for a long shot. Let's drive to the captain's house and hide the car somewhere and keep an eye on things."

The sun was shining but there was a stiff breeze blowing. "Not for long, then," said Agatha cautiously.

They set off again. Charles turned off a

country lane near the captain's house.

"I don't know how we're going to spy on her," complained Agatha. "There's that long drive past the farmhouse before you even get to the captain's house."

"Don't be defeatist. We'll think of something. Look," said Charles, "if we trespass on the captain's property and cross that field, we can hide in that stand of pine and get a good view of the entrance to the house."

"What if someone sees us! We'll be awfully exposed crossing that field."

"We'll risk it."

"What about the dogs?"

"They like me."

"What excuse are we going to give if we're caught?"

"We'll say we saw a rough-looking trespasser or one of those New Age travellers, and inspired by neighbourly duty we set across the field to clear them off."

"But — "

"Come *on*, Aggie!"

Reluctantly, Agatha set out next to him. Charles opened a gate into the field and shut the gate behind them. "We'll take the path around the edge of the field," he said. "No harm in that. It's when people walk across fields that the owners get mad."

They walked on, Agatha looking nervously all about her. She heaved a sigh of relief when they reached the stand of pine. Pine trees, thought Agatha; why couldn't they have been some thicker variety of tree? They stood in the shelter of one of the sturdier pines.

The entrance to the house was clearly visible. "Can I have a cigarette?" asked Agatha after half an hour.

"No," said Charles sharply. "Someone might see smoke rising from the trees and come to investigate."

"So how long are we going to stand here, freezing our assets?"

"Shhh! Someone's leaving."

As they watched, the tall figure of the captain emerged. He got into a dusty Land Rover, after, to Agatha's relief, putting the dogs in the back. They watched as he drove off down the drive and disappeared along the road, leaving only a black cloud of filthy exhaust to mark his going.

"Now what?" muttered Agatha. "Is that the exciting event of the day?"

"We wait to see if Lizzie Findlay makes a move."

Agatha craved a cigarette. If only she could quit and not be a slave to the beastly things. She peered up at the sky through the tops of the pines. "It's getting darker, Charles. Sun's gone in. Don't you think we should get out of here before it rains?"

"We waited this long. May as well wait a bit more."

After another three-quarters of an hour, Agatha felt cold and miserable. A sudden gust of wind rustled through the pines and she felt a drop of rain on her cheek.

"That's it," she said. "I'm off. I'm not waiting here to get pneumonia."

"Here she comes," whispered Charles.

Lizzie Findlay emerged wearing an old wax coat and with a scarf over her head. She got into a battered Ford Escort carrying a small case, which she put on the seat beside her, and after fumbling around a bit, put on a pair of driving glasses.

"Let her get down the drive," said Charles, excited, "and we'll follow her."

As soon as the Ford had disappeared, Charles grabbed Agatha's hand and forced her to run towards the car. Cold rain stung their faces, and as Charles had run straight across the ploughed field this time, Agatha's shoes were thick with wet mud by the time they got to the car.

"Which way did she go?" asked Agatha, climbing into the car and fastening her seat-belt.

"Don't know, but let's guess the Norwich road."

Charles drove off at great speed, and Agatha hung on as he screeched round the bends on the twisting road.

"Got her!" exclaimed Charles in triumph.

"Where?"

"Up ahead."

"I can't see."

"Three cars in front. I'll keep some cars between us in case she spots us."

They drove on steadily. "Yes, she must be going to Norwich. Let's hope we don't lose her in the city. At least it's not foggy."

Agatha was feeling depressed. Her feet were wet and muddy. Lizzie would probably go shopping and head straight home.

Lizzie drove straight into the centre of town, to the same car-park where Charles had stopped the night before. They found a space two rows behind where she was parking, and then got out. Lizzie was hurrying out of the car-park carrying the suitcase. They followed her along several streets until she stopped outside a betting shop, took out a key, unlocked a door next to the betting shop, which they guessed led to the flats above, and disappeared from view.

"'Curiouser and curiouser,'" quoted Charles. "Look, there's a café opposite with a free table at the window. We can sit there and keep watch."

The café owner cast a reproving look at Agatha's muddy shoes as they walked in. They ordered coffee and sat down at the table by the window. Time dragged on. They ordered more coffee.

Then they saw the door opposite open. "You were right!" said Charles excitedly. For the Lizzie who emerged was transformed. She was wearing a smart white raincoat and silk scarf. She was wearing sheer stockings and high heels. Her face was cleverly made up. She was by no means a beauty, but she looked a chic middle-aged woman instead of a downtrodden housekeeper. They paid for the coffee and followed her. She walked about, looking at the shops. She went into a department store. They followed. Lizzie bought some cosmetics. Then she went through to the lingerie department and bought a lacy bra and French knickers.

Carrying her purchases, and with Charles and Agatha in discreet pursuit, Lizzie returned to the door beside the betting shop and let herself in.

Once more Agatha and Charles took up watch in the café. The table at the window had been taken and so they took turns to stand up, craning their necks.

It was an hour before Lizzie emerged again as her old self, carrying the suitcase.

"Quick, we'll follow her," said Agatha, getting to her feet.

"No, sit down!"

Agatha reluctantly did as she was bid. "Why?"

"Because I think she's going home. I want to find out who rents that flat, if it's rented, and under what name."

They finished their coffee. Agatha was beginning to wish they had ordered some food, but at least, with all the waiting around, her feet were dry.

"We don't want the neighbours, if there are any neighbours, to report our visit," said Charles.

"I've done this sort of thing before," said Agatha eagerly. "I'll get a clipboard from a stationer's and some lined paper and say I am doing market research. Can you see from here? Are there any bells on the door?"

"Four, and an intercom."

"You wait here. Let's just hope there's someone at home."

She bought a clipboard at a nearby stationer's and then made her way back to the flats. Who should she be? Just vaguely market research. That would do.

There were no names on the bells, just flat

177

numbers. Only the fourth replied, an old woman's voice demanding shrilly, "Who is it? What d'ye want? If it's you kids again, I'll call the police."

"Market research," said Agatha into the intercom.

"Haven't got the time to answer a lot of damn-fool questions," came the reply.

"I'll pay for your time," said Agatha.

"How much?" Sharp and eager.

"Twenty pounds."

The buzzer went and Agatha pushed open the door and climbed up to flat 2. An elderly woman stood at the door, leaning on two sticks. "What's it about?" she asked.

She had an untidy, uncombed thatch of hair and two sharp beady eyes in a wrinkled face.

"Coffee," said Agatha.

"Coffee? I don't drink coffee."

I won't get far with this one, thought Agatha. Better go back to the café and wait to see if someone more amenable comes home to one of the other flats.

"Sorry to trouble you," said Agatha.

"Wait! Did you say twenty pounds?"

"Yes."

"Well, come in. I haven't got all day."

Agatha followed her into a neat living-room. A canary chirped in a cage at the window and two cats lay in front of a two-bar electric fire. Agatha repressed a shudder. In this old woman, she felt for a moment, she was looking at her future. "I'm Mrs. Tite. T-I-T-E."

Agatha dutifully wrote it down. "I don't drink coffee," said Mrs. Tite, "but my son does. Sit down." She lowered herself slowly and painfully into an armchair in front of the fire and Agatha took the one opposite.

"How many cups a day?" asked Agatha.

"About four or five."

Agatha dutifully wrote it down and then proceeded to ask a lot of questions about Mrs. Tite's son's coffee-drinking. "Now," said Agatha, "is there anyone else in these flats who would be prepared to answer questions?"

"There's George Harris and old Mr. Black — "

"I would prefer a woman. They're better at answering questions."

"Well, there's Mrs. Findlay, but I haven't seen much of her lately, or her husband, for that matter."

Agatha felt a pang of disappointment. This was just a flat the Findlays had bought or rented in town. She fished out a twenty-pound note and handed it over.

She rose to her feet. Mrs. Tite stroked and

folded the note and then tucked it in the pocket of her old woollen cardigan. "I'll see myself out," said Agatha. "Don't bother to get up."

"It's nice to see that," said Mrs. Tite, almost as if speaking to herself. "Love like that in middle age, and them married so long."

Agatha swung round, her hand on the door-handle. "You mean Captain and Mrs. Findlay?"

"Is he a captain? I didn't know that. Never used the title."

"I knew some Findlays," said Agatha slowly. "I must be confusing this Mr. Findlay with Captain Findlay. What does he look like?"

"Small, tubby man. High colour. Wore sporty clothes — hacking jacket, cravat with a horse-head pin in it."

"Thank you," said Agatha. She scampered down the stairs and across the road to the café, where she told Charles what she had found out, ending with "It couldn't have been Tolly, could it?"

"Sounds like it."

"But that's impossible! Why would a rich man like Tolly want to philander with someone like Lizzie Findlay?"

"Think about it. He's married to a hard

blonde who made it clear she only married him for his money. He chats up Lizzie, at first with the simple view in mind of ingratiating himself with her husband. What if it dawns on him that Lizzie finds him attractive? He's in love with the whole image of country life, and here's a real-live country lady who bakes cakes and makes jam — anyway, I'll bet she does. Maybe they meet by chance in Norwich one day and it takes off from there."

"And maybe she got a bottle of rose perfume from Rosie," said Agatha, "and that's what Lucy smelt in the bedroom." She shook her head. "It's too far-fetched."

"We can ask her."

"What?"

"We can just ask her. We'll try to get her on her own. Let's try this evening. I bet the captain goes out somewhere with his hunting cronies. Worth a try."

"I can't bear the idea of hiding out in those pines again."

"We'll go home and wait until after seven and then phone."

"But," said Agatha, as they walked to the car-park, "why on earth would she keep on the flat, continue to dress up, buy sexy underwear, if Tolly was the man. Tolly's dead."

"Maybe she found someone else."

"Highly unlikely."

"All will be revealed if we can get her alone."

When they got home, Agatha ate a hurried meal of sandwiches and phoned Rosie Wilden and asked her if she could buy some of her rose perfume.

"You're welcome to a bottle," said Rosie. "Next time you're in the pub, just ask."

"Thank you very much. I smelt some of your perfume just recently. Let me see, who was it? Ah, I believe it was Mrs. Findlay, Captain Findlay's wife."

"That'd be right," said Rosie. "Very partial to my perfume is Mrs. Findlay. I can't tell you how to make it because it's a family secret, but you just drop by and I'll let you have it."

Agatha thanked her and rang off. She went into the sitting-room, her face pink with excitement. She told Charles about the perfume.

"So," he said, "all we need to do is find Lizzie on her own."

Charles waited until seven-thirty that evening before dialling Lizzie's number. She answered the phone and when she said nervously that her husband was not at home, Charles said, "It's you I want to speak to. Can I come round?"

"I'm afraid it's not convenient."

"It's about your flat in Norwich."

There was a little frightened gasp, and then Lizzie said breathlessly, "I'll see you, but not here."

"Come here, then," said Charles. "It's Lavender Cottage, along Pucks Lane. Do you know it?"

"Yes."

"We'll expect you soon."

"You know what's bothering me," said Charles after he had told Agatha that Lizzie was going to call on them. "The fairies. I mean, the fairies have been totally forgotten in all this murder and mayhem."

"True. But if it was connected to the murder, why would anyone go to such elaborate lengths? Think of the risk, taking cheap bits of this and that."

"You forget about the Stubbs."

"I don't think the theft of the Stubbs had anything to do with it. Oh, there's the door-bell. Lizzie's quick."

But when Agatha opened the door, it was Hand who stood on the doorstep.

"Thought you would like to know," he said, stepping past her into the hall, "that whoever turned over your place wore gloves. Except for a set over near the fireplace. Had

183

any children round here?"

"No, none at all. In fact, I don't think there are any in the village other than Mrs. Jackson's."

"So we believe. My men have gone to see her with Detective Sergeant Carey. Just thought I'd check with you first."

"No, no children that I know have been round here," said Agatha, almost nudging him towards the door, desperate to get him to leave before Mrs. Findlay arrived.

"Right, then," he said, looking at her suspiciously. "I'll let you know how we get on."

"Good, good," said Agatha. "Many thanks."

How slowly he seemed to leave! Walking slowly along the side path past the hedge to where his car was parked.

Agatha waited nervously until she heard him drive off and then shot back into the house. "Phone Lizzie," she said to Charles. "She may have come round when Hand was here and got frightened off."

Behind her, the doorbell rang again, making her jump.

"That'll be Lizzie," said Charles.

SIX

†

Lizzie Findlay came in, blinking in the light. She looked small and faded and scared.

"Are you going to blackmail me?" she asked.

"Not at all," said Charles. "Take off your coat and come into the sitting-room."

He helped her out of her coat.

When they were all seated in front of the fire, Charles said, "We've found out you spent some time with Tolly, masquerading as his wife, in Norwich."

Lizzie went white. "You won't tell my husband!"

"No," said Agatha. "We just want to know what it's all about. We won't tell the police either."

"I suppose I'll have to tell you," said Lizzie, looking miserably down at her work-worn hands. "It started last year. Tolly was very nice to me and we talked a lot at those

185

interminable hunt dinners. After a bit, I began to tell him how awful my marriage was and he began to tell me how awful *his* marriage was and one thing led to another. My husband goes out a lot, and Tolly then came up with this idea of taking the flat in Norwich. My husband was going away to visit relatives in Canada for a month and he said he wouldn't take me. So that really started it, that month together. I was worried about Lucy finding out, but he said she didn't care a rap for him, only his money."

"Could the captain have found out?" asked Agatha. "Could he have killed Tolly?"

"I don't know," she said wretchedly. "I've worried and worried about it."

"We saw you in Norwich this afternoon," said Charles. "You were transformed — different clothes, make-up, all that. Is there someone else?"

"No," said Lizzie, "and there never will be now. I'm trapped for life. Tolly wanted to make out a new will . . ." Agatha flashed a triumphant look at Charles. "He wanted to leave everything to me. But I said Lucy would contest the will and there would be such a scandal. He kept saying he would get a divorce and I kept asking him if he'd told Lucy, but he always swore he would tell her soon. Then he said he would make a new will, leaving me the Stubbs, and that way I could sell it and be free of my husband."

"So there was another will!" cried Agatha.

Lizzie shook her head. "I don't think so. He said he'd made a new will on one of those do-it-yourself will forms from the stationer's, but why would he do that when, as far as he knew, he might outlive me?"

"But don't you see," said Agatha, excited. "Say he did make out another will and Lucy found it; she may have stolen the Stubbs herself to make sure you didn't get it."

"You haven't told us yet why you still go to that flat in Norwich and dress up," said Charles.

She gave a pathetic little smile. "The flat's paid up until the end of the year. You know how some transvestites parade around as women and that's all they do. I'm rather like that. Just for a little bit, I feel different, like I did with Tolly."

"You must have been devastated by his death," said Charles.

"At first I was terrified my husband had done it, but he's got such a temper, he would have let me know I had been found out. I was shocked and frightened by the murder, but the truth was that I think Tolly was just using me. I am related to the Earl of Hadshire on my mother's side of the family, and latterly all Tolly wanted was for me to engineer an invitation for him. I think the affair would have ended soon. At first I thought it was love because it's been years since I felt like a woman, but then there were all the excuses about how he couldn't tell Lucy just yet. I think he didn't want a divorce because of the alimony. He really didn't want her to get anything, and of course, he never expected to die so soon. Please don't tell the police any of this."

"We won't," said Charles. "But just suppose we somehow find the new will. Suppose we find the Stubbs. The police will have to know."

"In that case it wouldn't matter. I'd just leave and stay with my sister until the Stubbs was sold at auction. I should have left before, but that money would give me the courage to do it."

"Haven't you any money of your own?" asked Agatha.

"I'm afraid what little I have has nearly got used up secretly buying clothes."

"When we saw you going up to the flat, you were carrying a suitcase. Why didn't you just leave your good clothes at the flat?"

"I keep some at home in an old chest in my bedroom. We have separate bedrooms.

He never looks in mine. I have to have some nice things by me."

"Won't he let you wear pretty things?"

"No, he always finds fault with me. I think he likes me to look dowdy." Lizzie flashed a shy smile at Charles. "You men!"

Agatha bristled. Was this Lizzie as downtrodden and innocent as she seemed?

"Do you want a drink?" she asked. Charles raised his eyebrows in surprise because Agatha had barked out the offer.

"Oh, no, I must be getting back. So good of you both not to expose me." She stood up and smiled mistily at Charles, who said gallantly, "I'll get your coat."

He saw Lizzie out and came back into the sitting-room and surveyed Agatha, who was scowling into the flames.

"What got into you?" he asked.

"You may not have noticed, but Mrs. Oh-So-Innocent Findlay was beginning to flirt with you."

"Come on, Aggie, she's just a comfortable old-fashioned type of woman."

"Keep on thinking along those lines and you'll soon be getting a closer look at those French knickers she bought."

"So crude! If we all come back as something, Aggie, I swear you'll come back as a squashed fly on someone's windscreen. Stop

189

bitching, and let's have a look at what we've got. Now, say Tolly made that new will — forget about the murder — and Lucy pinched the Stubbs. What would she do with it?"

"You forget. She gets the insurance money. She can burn it if she likes."

"Right, so she can. But unless she murdered him, she wouldn't know she was going to inherit anything soon. So where do we go from here? Do you know, I feel guilty about Lizzie."

"Don't tell me you've fallen for her faded charms."

"I mean, I'm feeling guilty about us promising not to tell the police about that other will. Look at all the manpower they've got. Tolly would need to get two people to witness that will. I wonder who they were."

"We've forgotten about Paul Redfern, the gamekeeper."

"That's true. If Tolly was as much in love with all this countryside business as he seems to have been, then we would spend some time talking with the gamekeeper. It's too late to see him now. We'll try tomorrow."

The doorbell rang. "What now?" said Agatha, going to answer it. She came back followed by Hand.

"We found all the stuff hidden in a shed at the back of Mrs. Jackson's cottage. Her kids took it," he said.

"Who are they?" asked Agatha. "I've never seen them."

"There's four of the brats! Wayne, he's four; Terry, six; Sharon, seven, and Harry, eight. They said it was a bit of a joke. They'd hitched up an old set of Christmas-tree lights to a battery. I don't know how they got in your place, but they said a lot of people didn't lock their doors, or there was a window left open."

"What about the Stubbs?"

"They deny ever having been near the manor house. It doesn't help us with the murderer, finding the Stubbs. Taking little objects is one thing, but taking a large painting is another."

He looked at them narrowly. "Have you pair of would-be detectives discovered anything?"

"Nothing," chorused Agatha and Charles.

"I'm warning you. We need every bit of information we can get. I need not remind you of what will happen to the pair of you if I find you have been obstructing the police in a murder investigation by not passing on valuable information."

"Anything else?" asked Agatha sweetly.

"Nothing for the moment," he said grimly.

Agatha saw him out and then returned to Charles, looking uneasy.

"Let's hope Lizzie doesn't suddenly decide to talk to the police after all."

"Just so long as she doesn't say she talked to us first — and I don't see why she should — we'll be in the clear."

Agatha awoke the next morning and the first thought in her head was the forthcoming visit to the gamekeeper. The second thought was of James and she realized she was thinking about him less and less. Instead of being relieved that her obsession was fading, Agatha felt uneasy but did not understand why. The fact was that Agatha Raisin did not like to be left alone in the company of Agatha Raisin, and she obscurely sensed that without her obsession, there would be an emptiness in her brain, a cushion against reality. She rose and peeked round the door of Charles's bedroom. He was fast asleep, lying neat and composed.

Agatha went downstairs and dialled the Carsely vicarage number. The vicar answered. "Oh, it's you, is it?" he said grumpily. "Hang on." Agatha could hear him shouting, "It's that Raisin woman on the phone."

Mrs. Bloxby came on the line. "How are you getting on?" she asked.

"Not getting very far," said Agatha.

"Charles still there?"

"Yes."

"James isn't back yet. He must have been delayed."

"That's not why I was phoning," said Agatha defensively. "I just wondered how you were getting on."

"Pretty much the same as usual, and the pub stays the same as usual, you'll be glad to know. We've got a new woman in the village, a widow, a Mrs. Sheppard, very go-ahead. She headed the pub protest. I think she will be a useful addition to the ladies' society. Very good at organizing things."

Agatha felt a sharp pang of jealousy. "Sounds a bit like a bossy boots to me," she commented sourly. "I can almost picture her. Tweed and support hose and permed hair."

"No, Mrs. Sheppard is in her forties, blond, very smart. Great sense of humour. She's opened a florist's shop in Moreton and does the flowers for the church so beautifully."

I've got to get back, thought Agatha, before this harpy gets her hands on James.

"I thought you would be back by now," she realized Mrs. Bloxby was saying.

"I'm a bit fed up with things here," said Agatha. "I'll probably be back by tom— "

She broke off and gave a gasp.

"What is it?" demanded Mrs. Bloxby. "Are you all right?"

"Call you back." Agatha slowly replaced the phone. Through the half-open door, she could see the gilt edge of a picture frame.

She walked into the kitchen. Propped against the kitchen table was an oil painting of a man holding a horse.

"Charles!" screamed Agatha.

There was a muffled exclamation from upstairs. Then Charles could be heard hurrying down the stairs. He came into the kitchen. He was stark-naked. "Blimey," he said. "The Stubbs."

"It is. Isn't it?"

He moved forward. "Don't touch anything," yelled Agatha. "We'll need to phone the police. The painting was propped against one of the table legs."

"Just going to look at the back." Charles got down on all fours. The cats, thinking it was a game, weaved about him. He peered at the back of the picture. "There's an envelope taped to the back of it. Wait a bit; it says, 'Last Will and Testament of Terence Trumpington-James.' "

"That's Tolly."

"Yes, don't you remember, it said in the papers his name was Terence. He probably thought it was upper-upper to give himself a stupid nickname like Tolly. Call the police, Aggie."

"Get some clothes on, for heaven's sake."

Charles straightened up and went upstairs, as unselfconscious in his nudity as he was when he was dressed. Agatha phoned Framp, who said he would be round as soon as he had called headquarters.

Agatha then phoned Lizzie's number. The captain answered and kept demanding why Agatha wanted to speak to his wife and Agatha kept saying patiently that it was a church matter that only concerned Lizzie. At last the captain surrendered the phone to his wife.

"The will's turned up," said Agatha rapidly, "stuck on the back of the Stubbs. Yes, in our kitchen. I'm phoning to warn you that if that's the will you were talking about, the police will be round to see you. They won't think anything odd about Tolly leaving you the painting if he's still left everything else to his wife. You can just say it was a friendly gesture."

"I'm tired of it all. I'm going to tell the police the truth."

"Here they are now," said Agatha, hearing the doorbell.

She rang off. Charles came down the stairs, dressed, as Agatha opened the door.

It was Hand, Carey and Framp. "I was round at Mrs. Jackson's when I got Framp's call," said Hand. "Where is it?"

"Where I found it." Agatha led the way into the kitchen. "The will is attached to the back of the painting."

"You didn't touch anything?"

"No," said Charles. "I crawled on my hands and knees under the table and had a look at the back."

"Your whole place will need to be gone over again," said Hand. "We'll get the forensic boys over. Damn, I can't wait to see what's in that will, but I daren't touch anything."

It was a long morning for Agatha and Charles. After they had made their statements, they sat watching television, while police and forensic men in boiler suits went over the whole kitchen. "I hate these British schlock TV shows," said Charles, stifling a yawn. "The American ones are bad enough, but the British ones take things a rung lower."

"They're not so rock-bottom as the American ones," protested Agatha.

"It's just so un-British to wash all that dirty linen in public."

"Not anymore, it isn't. We've joined the touchy-feely races. I'm hungry," said Agatha. "I wonder how long they're going to be. I mean, if they don't want us, maybe they'll let us go out for something. I didn't tell you. I phoned Lizzie to warn her."

"Hope her husband doesn't horsewhip her."

"He might. She's going to bare her breast."

"I hope you warned her not to mention us."

"I didn't."

"Then we'll just need to pray she forgets about us or the wrath of Hand will descend on us. Wait here and I'll ask if they need us."

He came back and said, "Hand's on his road out with that will in a plastic envelope. Probably heading straight for Lizzie. The forensic people are going to be here for a few more hours, so we can go. But I would like to be a fly on the wall when Hand speaks to Lizzie!"

"Lizzie!" bellowed the captain. "Police!"
He turned to Detective Chief Inspector

Hand and Detective Sergeant Carey and said, "Can't you tell me what all this is about? Come into the study."

They followed him in. The captain positioned himself behind his desk. Hand and Carey remained standing.

There was a long silence and then they could hear Lizzie coming down the stairs. She walked into the study. She was wearing a smart red wool dress, and her hair was arranged in a soft style and her face was made up. The captain glowered at her. "What are you all dolled up like a tart for?"

She ignored him and turned to the detectives. "You wished to see me?"

Hand turned to the captain. "If we could see your wife alone . . . ?"

"Balderdash. There's nothing you can say to Lizzie you can't say to me."

"Let him stay," said Lizzie. All her terror of her husband had left her. She did not know if that will had been found, if there had even been such a will, but she had made up her mind that very morning to leave her husband.

"Very well," said Hand. "Please sit down." Lizzie sat neatly on the edge of a leather armchair by the fire and the detectives sat down on an old horsehair sofa.

"The Stubbs has been recovered," he

began. He went on to describe how it had been found in Agatha's kitchen and of the contents of the will. "The new will," he said, "was witnessed by Paul Redfern, gamekeeper, and Mrs. Elizabeth Jackson, cleaner, and I will be asking them why they told me nothing of this. As I said, it is pretty much the same as the old one except the Stubbs had been left to you, Mrs. Findlay."

"I must say that was jolly good of Tolly," said the captain.

Lizzie looked straight at him. "The Stubbs was left to me, not you. How soon can I get it, Inspector?"

"It will take some time. We need to get further ahead with this case and make sure no one is profiting from the murder. Where were you on the night Mr. Trumpington-James was killed, Mrs. Findlay?"

"I was here. I have no witnesses other than my husband and I do not know whether he was at home or not, for we have separate bedrooms."

"We will be speaking to your husband in a little while. Why would Mr. Trumpington-James leave you such an expensive painting?"

"That's easy," said the captain from behind his desk. "Tolly was mad about the hunt. Probably meant it for both of us."

"We were having an affair," said Lizzie, her carefully enunciated words dropping like stones into the gloomy study.

"Have you gone raving mad?" spluttered the captain.

"As I said," went on Lizzie with that deadly calm, "we were having an affair. He was going to get a divorce and I was going to get a divorce, but I don't think he ever really meant to divorce Lucy. He did not want to pay her alimony, you know."

"And how long had this been going on?"

"Over a year."

"And where did . . . er . . . you . . . where did your liaison take place?"

"Here and there," said Lizzie vaguely. She looked directly at her husband. "It really got going when you went to Canada. If you re-member, you wouldn't take me. You said it wasn't worth the extra expense."

The questioning went on. Did she know anyone with a cut throat razor? Had Mr. Trumpington-James mentioned any ene-mies?

And Lizzie answered every question with that same calm. When the questioning was finally over, she rose to her feet and said, "I am going upstairs to get my belongings and I would be grateful if you two gentlemen could wait here until I leave. I will tell you where I am going but I do not want my husband to have the address. He is a violent man."

"Violent enough to kill?" asked Hand.

Lizzie gave a little smile and sank the final metaphorical dagger right into her husband's breast. "Oh, yes," she said, and then she left the room.

"Now, sir," said Hand to the captain, "where were you the night Mr. Trumpington-James was murdered?"

The captain began to answer the questions in a dull voice. His colour was muddy and his voice flat and expressionless.

When they had finished questioning him, they went out into the hall, where Lizzie was sitting with two large suitcases. "Are we ready to go?" she asked brightly. "I've written my address down for you."

"I think you should accompany us to headquarters first," said Hand. "Detective Sergeant Carey will travel in your car with you."

"Too kind," murmured Lizzie. "Mr. Carey, if you could help me to my car with the cases? Thank you."

Agatha and Charles had spent a frustrating day. They had gone to call on the gamekeeper, only to find he had been taken off in a police car. "So maddening not to know anything," mourned Agatha. "Maybe the gamekeeper did it. Maybe Lucy was having an affair with the gamekeeper."

"How Lady Chatterley of her if she was," said Charles. "What about les girls?"

"You mean Harriet et al?"

"Exactly. Gossip runs round this village like wildfire."

"I know where she lives. Let's go."

Hariett was at home and her friends were with her, their husbands being, as usual, in the pub.

"Come in," said Harriet eagerly. "I was just thinking of phoning you. Such news! Fancy the Stubbs turning up in your kitchen!"

"How did you hear?" asked Agatha, following Harriet into her sitting-room, where Polly, Amy and Carrie were quilting.

"One of the policemen went into the pub for a pint and got talking to Rosie, and Carrie met Rosie on the village green and she told her. And guess what? Mrs. Jackson and Paul Redfern have been taken off in police cars. Do you think they did it?"

"No," said Agatha. "What reason would

they have? Gosh, I know. I bet they witnessed that will."

Four pairs of eyes goggled at her. Charles tried to give Agatha a warning kick but she was off in full gossipy flight. "There was a will attached to the back of the painting. I believe it leaves the Stubbs to Lizzie Findlay."

"That figures," said Polly.

"Why?"

"Well, I always said there was something going on there, didn't I? Last hunt dinner, I said to Peter I could swear they had been playing footsie under the table and he said, 'Don't be disgusting.' Wait till I tell him this."

"Oh, I don't think anything was going on," said Agatha.

"So loyal, so late," murmured Charles.

"I think the police have arrested Lizzie," said Amy.

"Why would they do that?" asked Charles.

"Sloppy Melton, who works on the farm the other side of the road from the captain's land, said he went up to see the man who runs the captain's farm, that's Joe Hardwick, and while they were talking, Lizzie comes out with suitcases and gets in her car, but there was a detective beside her and another following."

"If they'd arrested her," said Agatha, "she

wouldn't have been allowed to leave in her own car and with suitcases. I think she's left the captain."

"She wouldn't dare," breathed Carrie. "She was terrified of him."

"What if the captain thought his wife was having an affair with Tolly," said Agatha, and then coloured as Charles glared at her. "I mean, the whole idea's ridiculous, but he might have believed she was and gone and murdered Tolly."

"You don't know hunting," said Polly. "It's not a sport, it's a religion. The captain would have given Tolly his wife if it kept the funds coming in."

"But why on earth would Mrs. Jackson and the gamekeeper keep quiet about the will?" asked Agatha.

"That's easy," said Carrie. She smiled. She was wearing an attractive shade of pink lipstick and her eyes kept drifting to Charles.

"What's easy?" demanded Agatha crossly.

"It stands to reason that when it transpired, the solicitors had a will leaving everything to Lucy, and no mention was made of any other will, they would assume that was the only will."

"Or," said Harriet, "it could be because they were just told to put their signatures

204

down at the bottom of the will and didn't bother reading it. Why would they? Tolly would simply say he wanted their signatures, and they would sign, because he was the boss."

"What do you think of your fairies now?" asked Agatha, keeping her eyes on Carrie. "I mean, don't you feel rather silly finding out that it was only Mrs. Jackson's children?"

"There're strange things go on in old parts of Britain like this, but you wouldn't understand," said Polly dismissively. "Now you're here, Agatha, would you like to do some quilting?"

"We've got to get going," said Agatha. "Come along, Charles." She marched to the door of the sitting-room. She heard a burst of laughter and whipped round. Charles was creeping after her, touching his forelock. When he saw her glaring he said meekly, "Coming, missus. Don't beat me."

"Clown!" said Agatha, when they got outside.

"Don't order me around like a dog, Agatha. If you go on like that, they really will think I'm your toy boy."

"You can't be a toy boy," said Agatha nastily. "You're too old and you haven't got muscles."

"Let's go to the pub and see if we can pick

up any gossip." Charles set off rapidly across the village green, leaving Agatha to follow him.

When Agatha went into the pub, Charles was already at the bar, smiling at Rosie and ordering drinks. Agatha joined him. "There you are," said Charles. "One large gin and tonic for you. Oh, look, there's Framp over there. Let's join him."

The policeman was sitting alone at a corner table. As they walked to join him, Agatha was aware of three pairs of hostile eyes. While the wives were quilting, the husbands were back in the pub. She wondered about Henry Freemantle. He had threatened her and seemed to have a filthy temper. She must find out more about him.

Framp's glass was nearly empty, so Charles offered to buy him another. "Don't tell her anything until I get back with your drink," said Charles.

"I'm not allowed to tell anyone anything," said Framp moodily.

When Charles returned with the policeman's pint of beer, Agatha said, "I cannot understand why Mrs. Jackson and Redfern signed a will and didn't tell you about the new will."

"I can tell you that," said Framp, mellowed by the sight of the large pint. "It's simple. They said they didn't read the will, and as far as they were concerned that was the only will."

"Oh." Agatha was disappointed.

"Why do you think the Stubbs landed up in your house?" asked Framp. "And how did they get in?"

"Everyone seems to have keys to everywhere in this village," said Agatha.

Charles looked guilty. "I forgot to tell you, Aggie. I didn't lock up."

"What?"

"Fact. I meant to, but it slipped my mind. You'd gone up to bed first and I thought I'd watch a bit of television and then lock up, but I didn't."

"Still, he's got a point," said Agatha. "Why leave it with us?"

"I shouldn't be telling you this." Framp drained his pint and looked at the empty glass soulfully. "I'll get you another," said Charles quickly. He returned with a brimming pint and asked eagerly, "What aren't you supposed to tell us?"

"It's like this. Hand thinks it's odd that Mrs. Raisin here should have been writing a book called *Death at the Manor* in which a chap gets his throat cut with a razor, and bingo, we've got Mr. Trumpington-James with his throat cut. So he's beginning to think that no one put that Stubbs in your kitchen. You pair stole it and got rattled and decided to concoct a story about someone having left it there."

"That's ridiculous!" Agatha was pink in the face with outrage.

"He's looking into your finances to see if you were badly in need of money."

"This gets better," said Charles, looking amused. "So after we steal the painting, Tolly guesses it's us, and phones us up or something and we panic and nip up there and slit his throat with a safety razor which we just happen to have with us."

"Well, Hand says that county types like you, Sir Charles, often use an old-fashioned open razor."

"You know what I think," said Agatha. "I think someone panicked — not us — but knew the way Hand's mind was working and decided to get rid of a painting they didn't have the know-how to sell and make us look guilty."

"Far-fetched, that," said Framp.

"Thinking we're murderers is a damn sight more far-fetched," raged Agatha.

"Calm down," admonished Charles. "It's a hoot."

But Agatha was suddenly thinking of

James. Was he back? And how could she leave this village now that she was a murder suspect? She had not thought of him much, but now she did not have the freedom to leave Fryfam any time she wanted, he came rushing back into her mind.

"I've left my cigarettes," said Agatha, getting to her feet. "I'll nip home and get them."

"I'll get you some at the bar. Sit down," said Charles.

Amazement at this new generous Charles momentarily diverted Agatha, but as he returned with her cigarettes, she remembered she had her mobile phone in her handbag.

"Got to go to the ladies' room," she said brightly. "Where is it, I wonder?"

"Over there, under that sign saying 'Ladies'" replied Charles, looking at her suspiciously. Why was Agatha such a mixture of excitement and guilt?

Agatha went into the old-fashion ladies' room with its giant Victorian wash-basin, brass taps, and toilet with the huge brass pull-chain hanging down beside it.

She dialled Mrs. Bloxby's number. The vicar's wife answered. "Oh," she said, her voice a little distant. "How are you?"

Agatha told her about the finding of the Stubbs and then asked, "James back?"

"Well, yes, he came back today."

"Have you seen him?"

"As a matter of fact, he's just left."

"Did he ask for me?"

"He asked about the murder. He'd read about it in the newspaper."

Agatha clutched the phone tightly. "Nothing James likes more than a mystery. He'll be coming here, I suppose."

"He said he wouldn't be."

"What? Just like that? He said, 'I will not be going to Norfolk to see Agatha'?"

"I can't remember the exact words. I've got to go. Alf is calling me. 'Bye."

Agatha was so miserable that she joined Charles and Framp still holding the mobile phone in one hand. Charles stared at it, and Agatha blushed and thrust it into her handbag.

Mrs. Bloxby went into her sitting-room and sat staring at the fire. Was it a sin to lie when that lie was for someone's good? James Lacey had actually said, "I miss Agatha. I think I'll take a trip to this Fryfam place."

And Mrs. Bloxby remembered herself saying, "She's with Sir Charles." And the way James's face had gone a bit set and grim and how he had gone on to talk of other things.

But Mrs. Bloxby was fond of Agatha and

she felt that James Lacey would destroy Agatha's independent spirit. But, she thought miserably, she should not have told James about Charles. James would have gone to Fryfam and it would be obvious there was really nothing going on between Charles and Agatha. Anyway, there was an age difference of about ten years between them, thought Mrs. Bloxby naïvely, and that meant there would could not possibly be any affair. Mrs. Bloxby sighed. Telling James about Charles had been interference in Agatha's life and she had no right at all to interfere. If she had said, "Charles is over there with her," then that would have been all right because James must have seen Charles's name in the newspapers. But to say, "She's with Sir Charles," abruptly and in that *warning* way. That was lying. She heard her husband come in.

"What's up?" asked the vicar. "You look gloomy."

But she could no longer confide in him about Agatha. Alf did not like Agatha and would not understand her motives.

SEVEN

†

Agatha and Charles were glad that Framp had warned them of Hand's suspicions, so neither was particularly surprised when they found themselves borne off in a police car to headquarters.

They were interviewed separately. Under Hand's remorseless questioning, Agatha began to wonder if people actually caved in and confessed to crimes they had not committed, because he was almost making her believe she had done it. She was trying to control her temper, but was just about to crack and call him every name under the sun when they were interrupted. Tristan Tomley had arrived to represent both Agatha and Charles.

He joined Agatha at the table. Hand's questioning lost its belligerence and Agatha, glad of the support and wishing she had had the sense to demand a solicitor before

Charles had thought of it, answered all his questions calmly.

At last she read and signed a statement and was free to go. "You'll need to wait for Charles," said Tommers breezily. "Got to sit in on his questioning."

Agatha waited patiently on a hard chair by the front desk. She tried to conjure up a dream about herself and James, but the dream would not come. She remembered instead all James's coldness and anger, the way he would make love to her without saying a word. It's over at last, she told herself.

"Would you like a cup of tea?" asked the desk sergeant.

"No, thank you."

The desk sergeant straightened up and then groaned. "My joints are killing me," he said. "Don't you find when you get to our age that your knees and ankles ache the whole time?"

"No," replied Agatha curtly. That's all I need on this awful morning, she thought, to be reminded of my age by some fat-gutted copper whose joints would not ache so much if he lost some weight.

At last Charles appeared with Tommers. "Thank God that's over. Drink, Tommers?"

"Not me. I've got an appointment with a client. I'll be in touch."

Charles turned to Agatha. "Best smile," he said. "The press are outside. Some copper told me it's leaked out that we are helping the police with their inquiries."

"Isn't there a back way?"

"Oh, let's just face the music."

"Isn't a police car going to take us home?"

"That's an idea." Charles went up to the desk and asked if they could have a car to take them back to Fryfam.

"Detective Chief Inspector Hand ordered one, sir, and if I'm not mistaken, it's outside the door."

As Charles and Agatha exited, flashes blinded them and Agatha stumbled. Charles put an arm about her shoulders and got her into the police car.

When they arrived back at the cottage, Charles said, "Let's get the cats and clear off somewhere for the night and try to work out what we've got. If we stay here, the press will be hammering on the door any minute."

"Where will we go? A hotel won't take cats."

"We'll find one of those roadside motels. Don't mention the cats. We'll get a key and then just carry them in when no one is looking."

They hurriedly packed a couple of suitcases and put the cats in their travelling boxes and set out again. They found a motel on the outskirts of Norwich. It was a very expensive motel, and to Agatha's amazement Charles produced his credit card to pay for the bill. What had happened to this man, who was expert at "forgetting" his wallet?

They drove round to their room and carried the luggage and the cat boxes in. There were a sitting-room and a bedroom with one large double bed.

"We should have got one with single beds," said Agatha.

"Don't make a fuss," said Charles, who was kneeling on the floor and helping Hodge and Boswell out of their boxes. "It's an enormous bed. You stay on your side and I'll stay on mine. Put the cats in the middle if you fear for your honour."

"Should we tell the police where we are?" asked Agatha.

"I'll do that. Then we'd better eat something. We never seem to eat much these days."

Charles phoned the police and explained they were keeping away from the press.

"Let's wrap up and take a walk after we have something to eat. This place has a restaurant."

★★★

After they had eaten, they turned off the main road where the hotel was situated and walked along a country lane. A strong wind was blowing, sending the last of the autumn leaves swirling about their feet. Great ragged clouds chased each other across a stormy sky, driven by a north-eastern all the way from Iceland.

Agatha was glad she had put on boots and trousers. They walked a mile or two before returning to the hotel. When they went into their motel sitting-room, the cats ran up to Charles, purring and rubbing themselves against his legs.

"It's funny the cats should like you so much," said Agatha, taking off her coat. "They wouldn't ever go near James like that."

"They have good taste, those cats of yours."

"I thought you liked James."

"He's a man's man, to put it politely. If you had got married to him, Agatha, he would expect you to go on like his bat-man."

"He always respected my independence."

"When you were having an affair. Marriage is different. After the first fine care-less rapture is over, it all comes down to . . . 'What did you do with my socks?' Believe me, that one would have expected his shirts ironed and his dinner on the table."

"It's not going to happen," snapped Agatha. "I thought we were going to discuss this case?"

"Okay. Let's sit down and work it out." Charles took several sheets of motel stationery. "Now who and what have we got? Who is your prime suspect?"

"What about Captain Findlay? I'd like it to be him."

"So, does he steal the Stubbs as well?"

"Could be. If Tolly was loose-mouthed enough to tell the world the code for his burglar alarm, he may have confided in someone at the hunt about the Stubbs. Anyone else?"

"There's more going on in that village than we can even begin to imagine," said Charles. "Let's go back to the beginning. Lucy thinks her husband is having an affair with Rosie Wilden."

"But I thought Lizzie cancelled that idea out."

"Not necessarily. Why should Lizzie be the only one to have an affair with Tolly? Once he started philandering, he might have felt like spreading his wings."

"Then why should anyone murder him,

Charles? Lizzie was the one getting the Stubbs."

"Rats. Try again. You know, it's a pity Lucy has such a cast-iron alibi. Do you know what I think? I think we should nip back to the manor and try to see that gamekeeper."

"All right," said Agatha wearily. "We seem to have reached a dead end here. I'll feed the cats and give them some food. Better hang the DO NOT DISTURB sign on the door in case some maid comes in when we're out and frightens them."

The day was even colder when they set out for Fryfam, with a fiery-red sun sinking into black clouds. "Could almost snow," said Charles.

"Not yet, surely. It doesn't snow in Britain until January."

"Not anywhere else. This is Norfolk. But you're probably right. Isn't it funny, all those films and books about Christmas in England? It always snows. And yet I've never seen a white Christmas, except in places like Switzerland."

"Let's hope it doesn't snow here. That's all we need. I wonder how Lizzie is getting on. She'll have gone to that flat in Norwich. Will she have enough to live on?"

"She can always get a job. Do you re-member the captain said something about her wanting to be a secretary? If she's got shorthand and typing, she should get a job easily, despite her age."

"Maybe not. It's all computers these days. Let's not stay away too long."

"You're worried about your cats. Don't be. They're warm and fed and they've got each other for company."

As they approached the entrance to the manor-house drive, Charles said, "Let's get out and walk."

"Why?" grumbled Agatha. "It's freezing and I've walked enough for one day."

"If the police are about, I don't want them asking me any more questions. At the first sight of a uniform, we're off."

Still grumbling, Agatha got out of the car. They set off up the drive. "There's a road that leads off into the estate before we reach the house. The gamekeeper's cottage is probably along there," said Charles. "I wonder if Lucy's having a shoot. Waste of good birds if she's not. Pheasant all over the place."

"I don't think Lucy's the type to have any interest in country sports at all."

"She could charge good money for it. Look, there's someone over there."

A man was sitting at the wheel of a Land

Rover, smoking a cigarette. Charles approached him. "Do you know where we can find Paul Redfern's cottage?"

"Follow this road round that bend and you'll come to the cottage on your right."

"Thanks," said Charles. "Do you work here?"

"I do the maintenance," he said laconically.

"Police up at the house?"

"They were earlier but they've left."

Charles thanked him and he and Agatha walked on. Sleety rain began to sting their faces. "I wish we hadn't walked," mourned Agatha. "It's a long way back."

"If he's a friendly chap, we'll ask him to give us a lift to the gates. So here's the bend. Tolly must have spent some good money on this estate. It's well-maintained. Ah, here's the cottage. Funny how many of these estate cottages are mock Tudor. There's smoke coming out of the chimney. Good sign."

Charles knocked at the cottage door.

There was no reply. Night was falling fast and the rain was thicker and steadier. The wind suddenly dropped. There was no other sound but the rain pattering on the leaves of a laurel bush by the door.

"I think we've had a journey for nothing," said Agatha.

"I hate to think we've come all this way for nothing." Charles knocked at the door again. It slowly creaked open.

They looked at each other and then at the open doorway.

"Let's snoop," said Charles cheerfully. "At least we'll be out of the rain."

"I don't think . . ." began Agatha, but Charles was already walking inside.

She followed him into a minuscule hall. Charles opened a door to his right. Then he closed it again. "Don't look, Aggie. I'm going to be sick." He rushed outside.

But Agatha, overcome by curiosity, opened that door. What was left of the gamekeeper lay slumped in an armchair. Most of his head had been blown away.

Agatha clutched on to the side of the door. Then somehow she got herself outside. Charles was standing with his white face turned up to the falling rain.

Agatha sat down suddenly on the doorstep. She fumbled in her handbag for her mobile phone and called the emergency services and asked for the police and ambulance, wondering later why she had bothered to ask for an ambulance when there was nothing more could be done for Paul Redfern.

James Lacey switched on the six-o'clock

news. The pound was strengthening, the Government was being called upon to reduce interest rates, some fat Scottish member of the Cabinet was saying the Government knew what they were doing and James reached for the remote control to switch it off when suddenly the news changed to Norfolk. "Sir Charles Fraith and Mrs. Agatha Raisin were taken to police headquarters today to help police with their inquiries. Police have stressed that no charges have been made." Then there was a shot of Charles and Agatha. Charles's arm was protectively around Agatha's shoulders. They looked very much of a couple. James then switched off the television set and stared at the wall opposite. He felt angry and lonely.

Questions, questions and more questions. Then back to police headquarters to make their statements. Agatha and Charles were hungry and tired and very much shaken up by the time they were allowed back to their motel. They had picked up a pizza on the road to the motel and they ate that in silence.

At last Agatha said, "Why him?"

"Because he knew something," said Charles, "and now we may never know what that something was. I thought that mainte-nance man — Joe Simons — might have done it, but he'd been up at the houses, so the police say, just before we saw him, fixing taps. Let's go to bed and leave it all to the morning. You can use the bathroom first."

Agatha soaked in a hot bath and then put on a long brushed-nylon night-gown. She climbed into bed and picked up a book and tried to read to blot out the terrible sight of the dead gamekeeper.

Charles, having washed, joined her in the bed. He picked up a paperback from his side of the bed and began to read as well. Then he heard a muffled sob and looked at Agatha. Tears were streaming down her face. "I want to go home," she sobbed.

"Shhh, come here." He put his arms around her and held her close.

Agatha began to kiss him in a frenzied way. A gentleman would not take advantage of a situation, said some dim voice of con-science in the back of Charles's head, but he too was frightened and rattled, and so he did.

Agatha awoke in the morning and imme-diately the events of the night came flooding into her mind. She fished down at the bot-tom of the bed and retrieved her crumpled night-gown, pulled it over her head, and went off to the bathroom, feeling stiff and sore. Their love-making had been very energetic, almost as if they had been trying to thrash the horrors out of each other's minds.

But when she returned to the bedroom, feeling embarrassed, Charles said calmly, "At last. I thought you were going to spend all day in there."

He went into the bathroom. Agatha dressed in warm clothes. She fed the cats and checked their water bowls.

When Charles joined her, Agatha was at first grateful that he made no reference to their activities of the night before but then began to feel rather cross, thinking that he might at least say something.

But Charles, after making them coffee, said, "I think we should keep clear of Fryfam for a little. I think we should go and see if we can talk to Lizzie."

"Why?"

"God knows. But she did have an affair with Tolly. She must know a lot about him. There must be something she can tell us."

"All right," Agatha muttered, not looking at him.

"I'm not going to be lovey-dovey with you, Agatha Raisin," said Charles. "But in your moments of passion, you might have the decency to remember my name."

"What?"

"'Oh, James, James,'" mocked Charles. "I'll see you in the car."

Agatha felt herself blushing all over. If only she could just run away and forget about the whole thing.

Lizzie Findlay was at home.

She let them into a small neat flat. "How's Tommy?" she asked.

"Tommy?" asked Agatha.

"My husband."

"I don't know," said Agatha. "Why?"

"I can't help wondering how he's getting on without me," said Lizzie. "He can't cook, you know." She flashed a timid smile at Charles. "You men are so hopeless."

"Charles cooks," said Agatha. "We keep wondering and wondering who killed Tolly — and now Paul Redfern."

"It's a nightmare," said Lizzie. "Who would want to kill Paul?"

"He might have known something. He might have been blackmailing someone," said Charles. "He witnessed that will."

"It all comes back to Lucy," mourned Agatha. "Such a suitable subject."

"But she's got an alibi. Tolly always said it suited Lucy very well being married to him." Lizzie began to walk up and down the room. "He said when they'd had a row she would punish him by going out and buying something expensive. I said, why didn't he just stop her credit cards, take control of the money. Tommy never allowed me a credit card. Tolly sort of waffled on and said he would do something about it. I don't think near the end that Tolly cared for me at all. He just liked the excitement of cheating on his wife. And I'll tell you something else. At the last hunt dinner before he died, he entered with Lucy on his arm. She was wearing a Liz Hurley sort of gown, slit up both sides and with a plunging neckline. All the men were goggling, and do you know, I think Tolly was *proud* of her."

"How are you managing for money?" asked Charles.

"I have a little left from an inheritance and I've applied for a job in a supermarket. They take older people."

"Did Tolly talk about enemies?"

"No, he was too much of a people-pleaser in the country to annoy anyone."

"What about his past life? Anything there?"

She shook her head. "Not that he told me. I do hope Tommy's all right."

"Why should you care about your husband?" asked Agatha curiously. "He seemed to have led you a dog's life."

"It was a busy life," sighed Lizzie. "I seemed to have such a lot to do during the day. There was the cleaning and cooking and baking things for the church sales and so on. I'm not used to being idle. Perhaps if I get a job, things won't be so bad."

"Are you sure your husband didn't kill Tolly?"

"He might have done it, but he wouldn't have killed Paul. He admired Paul. Said he was a first-class gamekeeper."

Agatha studied Lizzie covertly. Could Lizzie have murdered Tolly? But it would take strength to creep up behind a man and slit his throat. Tolly must have heard some sound and come out of his bedroom to investigate. Still, one arm around his neck, pull his head back, and zip! She felt that underneath Lizzie's calm exterior were layers and layers of undiscovered territory.

Lizzie saw Agatha watching her and said, "If you don't mind, I would rather you left. I'm rather busy."

"Doing what?" asked Agatha.

"Come on, Aggie," said Charles.

"So what did you make of that?" asked Agatha when they were outside. "I suppose you fell for that meek-housewife routine."

"On the contrary, I kept thinking she might make a good murderess."

"I wondered about that. But it would have taken strength to bump off Tolly."

"Did you see her arms and hands? She was wearing that short-sleeved blouse and she's got strong arms and hands. And if she killed Paul — well, I bet she knows how to use a shotgun."

"I've not really had time to sit down and think it through," said Agatha.

"What, like Poirot? Going to exercise the little grey cells, Aggie?"

"Don't sneer," said Agatha. "Let's go back to the motel and try to work things out again."

After a welcome from the cats, they sat down with sheets of paper. "Let's not talk," begged Agatha. "I think each of us should try on our own and then we'll compare notes."

She wrote down everything they had found out, little though it was, and then reread what she had written. She then glanced across at Charles. He was chewing the end of a pencil and scowling down at his notes. Agatha felt a sudden spasm of lust and then shuddered. Never again. There was something so demeaning about casual sex.

Perhaps it was because she belonged to the wrong generation. Somewhere she had read that young women didn't suffer from the same pangs of guilt and remorse. Affairs. Lizzie's affair with Tolly. Lucy had suspected something. If Lucy had found out, then she could have had grounds for divorce and get a good settlement, too. What was Lucy really like? Agatha had put her down as a bimbo. But people were never that simple. That was the bad habit of stereotyping people. It stopped one from looking underneath. Someone had feared her and Charles, someone had been worried that they might have found out something. But who could that have been? Nothing had been taken. There had been no attempt to make it look like a robbery. Which argued that someone had been very confident. No, that was wrong. A confident person wouldn't have been frightened enough to break in. And why leave the Stubbs with them?

Agatha wrote LUCY in block capitals and stared at it. But Lucy had been away. All right. Indulge in a flight of fantasy. Lucy had learned about the will and had taken the Stubbs. Something tips her over the edge. Tolly wants a divorce. Okay, what would upset her about that, provided he offered a settlement? But what if she wanted it all?

So she kills Tolly. But why Paul Redfern?

"Got anything?" asked Charles.

"Let's swap notes," said Agatha.

She started to read Charles's neat script. He had written, "Why is Mrs. Jackson so loyal? Is Lucy paying her to keep her mouth shut? Blackmail? But Lucy couldn't have committed the murder."

"Is that all?" asked Agatha.

"Mmm? Wait a bit, till I read yours. You don't mention Lizzie or Captain Findlay."

"That's because Lizzie said the captain admired Paul."

"But I've got an interesting idea in blackmail. That would explain the return of the Stubbs."

"I don't see why."

"Look," said Charles, tapping Agatha's notes with his pencil. "Let's think about blackmail. Mrs. Jackson and Redfern know about that other will. They witnessed it. Say, Redfern tells Lucy. She nabs the painting. Something then happens to make her kill her husband. Up pops Redfern and says, 'Unless you pay me, I'll talk about that other will.' I've got the loot, I don't need the painting, thinks Lucy, and I'm not going to be blackmailed, so she dumps it on us. Redfern then ups and says, 'Pay up or I'll tell the police you stole that painting,' so

230

she blasts him with a shotgun."

"I wish she didn't have such a cast-iron alibi." Agatha suddenly thought of James. Why hadn't he phoned? Perhaps he was trying even now.

"The heat from the press should be off by now," she said. "Let's go back to the cottage. Whatever clues we need are in Fryfam."

Charles sighed. "I must admit, I'm tired of this motel room. But the press will still be snooping around. It's too hot a story for them to drop. We'll leave in the morning."

Agatha felt nervous about going into the cottage when they got back. She stood outside until Charles had checked every room for either dead bodies or would-be assailants under the bed.

Finding it was safe, Agatha let out the cats into the garden. Barry Jones was raking up leaves. "Hope you don't mind," he called. "I borrowed the key from Mrs. Jackson and let myself into the kitchen for a cup of tea."

Agatha walked down the garden to join him. "Do you always call your mother Mrs. Jackson?"

"Only to folks who don't know the score. It confuses people, us having different names."

"What was your father like?"

231

"Dunno. He scarpered right after I was born."

"Chatting up the garden Adonis?" asked Charles when Agatha came back into the kitchen.

"He is incredibly good-looking, isn't he?" said Agatha.

"Now there's a real toy boy for you."

"I might consider it," snapped Agatha. "What are we going to do now?"

"I'm going to watch something stupid on television. If I keep thinking about it and thinking about it and thinking about it, I'll never get anywhere."

Agatha retreated to her bedroom and shut the door. She waited until she could hear the sounds of the television set downstairs, then took out her mobile phone and called Mrs. Bloxby.

"Oh, dear, what has been happening to you?"

There was a ringing at the doorbell downstairs. "Wait a minute," said Agatha. She put her head round the bedroom door. "Press," came Charles's voice. "I'm not going to open it."

Agatha retreated into the bedroom. "That was the press," she said to Mrs. Bloxby.

"Is it not getting a little dangerous for you to be there?" asked Mrs. Bloxby. "You always stir things up and then someone tries to hurt you."

"I'm safe for the moment, with the village crawling with police and press. How's things in Carsely?"

"Very quiet."

"James getting on all right?"

"Yes, he and that Mrs. Sheppard I told you about have struck up a friendship."

"Oh, the pushy blonde."

"Now, now, she's not at all pushy and very amusing. What's been happening? I saw you and Charles on the television news."

Agatha told her all about the new will, Lizzie and the captain, and the dead end they had reached in looking for motives and suspects. Then she told her the whole business in detail from the beginning.

Agatha ended up by saying, "We'll maybe have to look further. I mean, it could have been any member of the hunt, for all I know. And that Lizzie, I'm beginning to think she is a bit of a minx. She can't be all that downtrodden and crushed. She was even flirting with Charles."

"And did that annoy you?"

"Of course not. I'm not interested in Charles. Still, it was a bit odd."

"How was the Stubbs left in your house? I mean, how did they get in?"

233

"Charles forgot to lock up."

"And the time before, when the place was searched? Any signs of a door or window being forced?"

"No, someone must have had a key."

"Does anyone who might be involved in this work at the estate agents'?"

"Yes, Amy Worth. But it can't be her."

"Why not?"

"What motive?"

"There seem to be a lot of secret passions in that village. Blame it on the awful Norfolk weather. Once the summer visitors leave, those women can have little else to do but make mischief. Satan finds some mischief for idle hands to do."

"Quite. Still, you've got a point."

"And doesn't that cleaner have a key?"

"Yes, but she only got one recently."

"But before the return of the Stubbs?"

"I suppose so," said Agatha. "Anyway, thanks. You've given me some points to think about."

"Any message for James?" asked Mrs. Bloxby, feeling contrite.

"Doesn't seem much point now he's got that paragon of all the virtues to entertain him."

James was sitting with Mrs. Sheppard in

Carsely's pub, the Red Lion. Despite the chill of the day, she was wearing a sleeveless red chiffon dress. Her blond hair was smooth and shiny but she kept tossing it about like a model in a shampoo advertisement. James could feel himself becoming more and more bored. If only it were the prickly irritating Agatha Raisin opposite. Agatha could be infuriating, but she was never, ever boring.

Agatha told Charles what Mrs. Bloxby had said, but omitting any mention of James. "So many people," mourned Charles. "So many suspects. I feel like going home. What about you? The police can't really keep us here."

But Agatha suddenly did not want to go back to Carsely. In her imagination, James was already engaged to Mrs. Sheppard. And she did not want to be left on her own without Charles.

"We may try a little longer." Charles was putting his coat on. "Where are you going?" asked Agatha.

"I'm going to buy a couple of bolts, one for the back door and one for the front. While I do that, why don't you pop down to the estate agent's and have a word with Amy?"

"All right, but I don't think that woman's

got much more in her mind than quilting and church affairs."

Agatha set out. The wind was cold and the ground was frozen and slippery. She made her way cautiously across the village green and then heard herself being hailed from the pub. Rosie Wilden was standing outside, waving to her. Agatha walked back to join her. "Come in, Mrs. Raisin, dear. I've got a bottle of my perfume for you."

"Thanks," said Agatha, following her into the darkness of the pub. "We're not open yet," said Rosie. "Where are you off to?"

"I was just going to call on Amy Worth at the estate agent's."

"You'd better hurry. They close at five-thirty and it's nearly that. Here's your perfume."

"Thanks a lot. Are you sure I can't pay you for it?"

"My pleasure."

Agatha hurried off, thinking that she must get Rosie something to repay her for the perfume and for that free meal.

Amy was just locking up when Agatha came hurrying up.

"What's happened?" she asked.

"Nothing more," said Agatha. "I think enough has happened already. I just wanted a chat."

"I live next to Harriet. Walk round with me and we'll have a cup of tea."

Amy's house was smaller than Harriet's, a trim 1930s bungalow with pebble-dashed walls, looking out of place among the other older houses of Fryfam.

"Is your husband at home?" asked Agatha, following Amy into her kitchen.

"No, Jerry's working late. Sit down. Tea? Coffee? Something stronger?"

"Coffee will be fine. Mind if I smoke?"

"I do, actually."

"Oh, well." Agatha put away the packet of cigarettes she had taken out of her pocket. "I'm at my wits' end trying to figure out who murdered Tolly, and Paul Redfern."

"It's really not your job," said Amy. There was a loose thread hanging down from her droopy skirt. Agatha was wondering whether to tell her about it when Amy giggled and said, "Now tell me all about you and Sir Charles."

There was a decidedly prurient gleam in her pale eyes.

"Nothing to tell," said Agatha defensively. "I mean, you all seem to be up to such shenanigans in this village, you probably think everyone else is at it." A quick memory of Charles's well-manicured hands on her body came into her mind, and to banish it she said jokingly, "Take you, for instance. I know all about you!"

Amy had just lifted up the kettle to fill two coffee mugs. She dropped the kettle and jumped back as boiling water went all over the kitchen floor.

"You bitch," she hissed. "How did you find out? It's that Jackson woman, isn't it?"

Agatha stared at her in amazement. A steely wind outside rattled the bare dry branches of a tree against the window. Somewhere a dog barked and children laughed. The mysterious Jackson children?

"Sit down," said Agatha. "Look, I'll help you mop up. I was teasing you. I didn't know. But I want to know now. But come to think of it, I don't need to know who it is unless it's Tolly."

Amy slumped down at the kitchen table, her feet in a pool of water.

"I may as well tell you. It's got nothing to do with any of this. It's Mr. Bryman."

"Your boss, the estate agent?" asked Agatha, amazed as she thought of the damp and unlovely Mr. Bryman. "Where does this affair take place? Here, when Jerry's away?"

"No, Cecil — that's Mr. Bryman — said it was too dangerous. In the office on a quiet day."

Where? Agatha wanted to ask. On the

desk? Behind the filing cabinets? The mind boggled.

"You won't say anything," pleaded Amy. "It's just a bit of fun."

"No, but where does Mrs. Jackson come into all this?"

"She found out. She used to clean the office one morning a week. But she came in one evening and caught us at it. She said she had to call at the school in the morning because one of her kids was in trouble, so she'd decided to do it the night before. She has a key, of course."

"I'm beginning to think Mrs. Jackson has keys to places all over the village," said Agatha. "Here, let me help you mop up this water."

"It's all right. I'll do it."

"So what did Mrs. Jackson say?"

"Nothing then. But she dropped in when Cecil was out one day. She began to hint that it would be awful if my husband knew. I don't know whether she meant to blackmail me or not, but just in case, I said, 'You'd best be careful what you say, I've got the tape recorder running, and if you blackmail me I'm going straight to the police.' I hadn't got the tape recorder running, but she didn't know that. She got very flustered and said she couldn't understand why I could think such an evil thing. She was a God-fearing woman, and yak, yak, yak. Oh, God, there's Jerry back. You'd better go. He's never forgiven you for that evening in the pub."

"I'm off." Agatha smiled weakly at Jerry as he came into the kitchen and he responded with a glare.

As she walked across the village green, her mind was buzzing with ideas. Must tell Charles. Promising not to tell anyone didn't include Charles.

Somehow, the solution to both murders was there in the back of her head. It was only a matter of looking at things differently.

EIGHT

†

Charles was lying on the sofa with the cats on his lap when Agatha burst into the sitting-room. "I think I've got something," cried Agatha, "but I don't know what it is."

Charles gently placed the cats on the floor and swung his legs down and sat up.

"Sit down, Aggie, take off your coat, and stop your eyes bulging and I'll get you a drink."

Agatha sat down on the sofa. Charles handed her a gin and tonic and then poured a whisky and water for himself. "Begin at the beginning," said Charles. "What did Amy say to get you so excited?"

Agatha carefully recounted everything she had found out. "Now that is interesting," said Charles. "Not about her affair, which doesn't bear thinking about, but about Mrs. Jackson. Let's say Mrs. Jackson is a blackmailer. Who does she blackmail?"

"Lucy," said Agatha. "Back to square one. And yet, I've a feeling we've been looking at things the wrong way round."

"Could be. Mrs. Jackson witnesses the new will. She tells Lucy. Forget for a moment about Lucy's alibi. She subsequently blackmails Lucy."

"So what's that got to do with Paul Redfern?"

"I don't know. Stop asking awkward questions and let me think."

They went over it and over it without getting any farther.

At last, they decided to eat and have an early night. But Agatha found she could not sleep. How odd, that affair of Amy's. Agatha began to wonder if she, Agatha, was one of those romantic prudes, always living in dreams. Maybe it wasn't just the young who could indulge in casual sex without conscience. But perhaps Amy was in love with her Cecil.

Her thoughts turned to Lucy. Lucy had suspected her husband was having an affair with Rosie Wilden. Only it wasn't Rosie Wilden, it was Lizzie. But then Lucy had almost seemed to want to forget she had ever mentioned the subject. And why had Lucy asked her, Agatha, to investigate her husband in the first place — a woman, a stranger who only claimed to have had some success as a detective? A blind? Why?

What if, just what if, *Lucy* was having an affair? Let's turn it on its head. Lucy is having an affair. She wants the money and she wants to get away with her lover. She gets this lover to bump off her husband. First she hears about the will from Mrs. Jackson and steals the Stubbs. Okay, so far, so good. What prompts her to get rid of it when the insurance money would add to what she's going to get? And what about Paul Redfern? He was murdered *after* the will was found. Maybe he knew something. Maybe he'd decided to try a spot of blackmail himself.

Agatha groaned and got out of bed. She went into Charles's room and shook him awake.

"Agatha," he said, smiling up at her. "I thought you would never ask."

"It's not that, Charles. Look, I'm nearly on to something."

He sighed and got out of bed. "Let's go downstairs and see what we can work out."

In the sitting-room, he piled logs on the red glow of ash in the hearth. "So let's hear it," he said.

Agatha went over her muddled thoughts, ending up with "So you see, if Lucy had a lover, it would all fall into place."

"I never liked that Jackson woman," said Charles. "Now if Lucy had a lover, the trouble is it could be a member of the hunt that we haven't even thought about."

Agatha sat forward in the armchair. "Wait a bit. Hunt members would mostly have money. So Lucy could just divorce Tolly and marry her lover."

"Maybe he's married already."

"Then there would be no point in murdering Tolly."

"True. So is it some village swain?"

They looked at each other.

"What about the gardener, Barry Jones?" exclaimed Agatha. "And he's Mrs. Jackson's son. Mrs. Jackson goes on about how loving Lucy and Tolly were and yet by all accounts Lucy hated her. But if Lucy was having an affair with Barry Jones, her son, she would cover up for her. Barry married to the wealthy Lucy would mean money for Mrs. Jackson. So let's suppose that Paul Redfern knows something and tries to blackmail Lucy and she tells Mrs. Jackson and Barry shoots him to keep him quiet. Should we phone the police?"

"Come on, Aggie. They'd think we were mad. What proof have we that Barry was having an affair with Lucy?"

"Someone must know in this village," said

Agatha. "It's such a little world. Barry worked as gardener up at the manor. They could have carried on an affair easily, what with Tolly being away a lot romancing Lizzie. Tolly spent a whole month with Lizzie. What excuse did he give Lucy, or did he just have a fling with Lizzie during the day and return at night?"

Charles sighed. "There's not much more we can do tonight. I tell you what. Let's try to have a word with Rosie Wilden in the morning, before the pub opens. I bet she knows all the gossip."

Agatha awoke to a white morning. There had been a heavy frost the night before. Everything glittered in weak sunlight. Even the cobwebs on a bush outside the kitchen door were perfectly rimed in frost.

The cottage felt like an icebox. Agatha lit the Calor gas heaters and put on a pot of coffee before waking Charles. She saw no reason why Charles should lie in bed long enough to wake up to a warm house. Agatha Raisin did not like to suffer alone.

"It all seemed so logical last night," mourned Agatha. "Now it seems like a load of old rubbish."

"Never mind. We'll check out Rosie, *and* we'll eat a proper breakfast before we go."

They set out an hour later. The sun was now a small red eye of a disc high above, behind a thin layer of hazy cloud. "I don't care how many more murders there are," said Charles. "I'm going to be home for Christmas."

"Christmas," echoed Agatha. "It looks like a Christmas card here already."

"I suppose if we knock at the front door of the pub, no one will answer," said Charles. "Rosie might think it's some drunk. We'll try the back."

They went along a passage at the side of the pub, through a gate, and into a back garden dotted with chairs and tables. "She must use the garden in the summer," said Agatha.

There was a clattering of dishes from the kitchen. Charles knocked at the door. Agatha had a brief hope that a messy Rosie would answer with her hair in curlers, but the Rosie who answered the door looked like any man's dream of femininity. Her thick blond hair was in a knot on the top of her head. She wore a frilly apron over a crisp cotton blouse and tailored skirt and held a mixing bowl under one arm.

"Come in," she said. "I was just about to take a break from my baking." The large kitchen was comforting and warm and smelt of baking and spices. An elderly woman rose as they entered. "My mother," said Rosie.

"I'll just go upstairs," she said, gathering up a bundle of knitting.

"Sit down," urged Rosie. "I've got some coffee ready."

"We came to see if you knew any gossip," began Agatha, plunging right in. Charles thought, as he often did, that Agatha Raisin had all the subtlety of a charging rhino.

"Well, I don't know about that, Mrs. Raisin, dear," said Rosie, pouring two cups of coffee into French-type coffee bowls and then lifting a tray of hot scones out of the Aga. "I hear a lot of gossip but I find it safer to forget about it, if you take my meaning."

She put a pat of golden butter on the table, and tilted the scones onto a plate. "Help yourselves," she said. "Let me see, I think a pot of my black-currant jam would go nicely with those."

She sat down with them and smiled slowly and warmly at Charles. Somehow that smile irritated Agatha, so she crashed tactlessly on. "Was Lucy Trumpington-James having an affair with anyone in the village?"

There was a veil over Rosie's blue eyes now, like the cloud veiling the sun. After a little hesitation, she said, "If she was, then it was her business, if you take my meaning."

"Come on, you can tell us," urged Agatha.

"Don't reckon as how I can. I'd have no customers if I talked about folks' private lives."

"But surely Lucy didn't drink in the pub?"

"No, but there's others who do."

"Meaning she had a lover and he drank in the pub," exclaimed Agatha. "That narrows the field. It's really only the ordinary villagers who drink in your pub, not the members of the hunt."

"Now you're going on as if only rich aristocrats hunt," chided Rosie. "Mr. Freemantle, Mr. Dart and Mr. Worth all hunt. So does Mrs. Carrie Smiley. Real attractive she looks in her hunting costume, too."

Agatha leaned forward. "But you *know*."

"I don't know anything," said Rosie sharply. "You're letting your coffee get cold."

Charles spoke. "I think you left the cats out in the garden, Agatha, and the frost will hurt their paws. You'd better go and let them in." He looked blandly at Agatha and Agatha took it that he meant that as she was getting nowhere, she'd best leave it to him.

She affected a look of dismay and said,

"I'm sorry, Rosie. I forgot about the cats. Got to go."

Outside, she wondered what to do. She could not lurk around outside the pub waiting for Charles. Yet, on the other hand, she was reluctant to return to the cottage. She decided to walk out of that village to the lake, to see if she could clear her thoughts and put them in some sort of order.

As she entered the road leading out of the village, she marvelled how quiet the day was and how very still.

The pine trees on either side looked ready for Christmas with their frosting of white. On she went until she crested the hill again and looked out across the great vast flat silence of Norfolk.

When she got to the lake, she sat down on a flat rock again. Ice had formed on the edges of the lake. She wondered if people skated on it when it was completely frozen over. What if they had skating parties, with Rosie handing out glasses of mulled wine and mince pies? And what if a visitor like herself should come across such a scene? She would envy them, thinking they all led a safe, typically English sort of life, unaware of all the passions that lurked beneath the surface. A little breeze rippled across the glassy waters of the lake and she shivered and rose

249

to her feet again. She could not go any further in her thoughts without some proof. It was as she approached the gates to the manor that Agatha suddenly remembered the maintenance man. What was his name? Joe something. And would a maintenance man have a cottage on the estate? She turned up the drive and then took the fork which led to Redfern's cottage. As she rounded the bend, she could see police tape fluttering in front of it and Framp on duty outside, stamping his feet and rubbing his arms to keep the cold at bay.

Agatha retreated. She did not want to be caught by Hand talking to the policeman. She reached the fork of the road again when a small truck stopped beside her. She recognized the maintenance man. "Looking for something?" he demanded. "The police don't want any press or trespassers around here. Wait a bit, I saw you when Paul was shot."

"I found the body," said Agatha.

"So what's your business here? Mrs. Trumpington-James is sick of snooping busybodies."

Agatha was about to say she had wanted to ask him a few questions but decided against it, he looked so suspicious and truculent.

"I am a friend of Lucy Trumpington-James," she said haughtily. "I took the wrong road to the house."

"That way," he said, jerking a thumb over his shoulder. Agatha walked towards the house. She stopped a little way away from the truck and looked back. He was still parked there and watching her in his rear-view mirror. She would need to call on Lucy.

The windows of the house were red in the sunlight, like so many accusing red eyes staring at her.

She rang the bell and the door was immediately opened by Lucy. She was wearing a thick Arran sweater and jeans. Her hair was tied up in a chiffon scarf and her face was clean of make-up, making her look younger and softer.

"I saw you coming up the drive," said Lucy. "I could do with an excuse to stop work and have a drink."

Agatha walked into the hall and looked at the packing cases. "Are you leaving already?"

"I can't," said Lucy. "Not with coppers all over the place refusing to let me until the murder is solved." She walked into the drawing-room and Agatha followed her. "What'll you have to drink?"

"Gin and tonic, please."

"I don't have ice."

"Doesn't matter," said Agatha. "The day's cold enough."

Lucy handed her a drink and then poured herself a large brandy. "You can smoke if you like," said Lucy. "I've started again."

"Great," said Agatha, taking out a packet of cigarettes. "I just called to see how you were getting on."

"Not very well, to tell you the truth. I thought it would all be so simple. Sell up here, get out, move back to London. But the rozzers are hell-bent on making sure I had nothing to do with the murder."

Agatha took a sip of her drink. Then she asked, "Why would they think that?"

"Because I inherit. One detective had the cheek to say it was nearly always the husband or wife. Would you believe it?" Lucy nervously puffed smoke. "It was all setting down nicely and then the fools had to go and shoot Paul."

"The fools?" asked Agatha.

"Poachers. That's what I told the police. Paul's had several of the locals up in court and they don't forgive easily around here."

"Did you know Tolly was having an affair with Lizzie?" Agatha did not feel any longer that she owed Lizzie any loyalty. Besides,

Lizzie had left her husband in a police car complete with suitcases, so she must have told them about the affair, or so Agatha justified it to herself.

"No, isn't that a laugh?" said Lucy bitterly. "Lizzie Findlay, of all people, and I'm expected to go on like a nun. I wondered why Tolly had given up sex with me. Now I know. I never thought he was having an affair."

"But you did," protested Agatha. "You asked me to find out."

"Oh, that. I thought he'd been with Rosie. Damn, I could just have divorced the old bastard and taken him to the cleaner's. His sister turned up at the funeral, making a scene."

"I didn't know the funeral had even taken place!"

"The police kept it quiet and so did I. As fed up with the press as they are. Crematorium in Norwich. Have another drink?"

"I haven't quite finished this one." Lucy rose and took the glass from Agatha. "I'll freshen this up. I don't like drinking alone."

"Do you think Lizzie's husband might have murdered your husband?"

Lucy handed Agatha a brimming glass and then topped up her own with more brandy.

She slumped down in her chair again. "Who cares?" she said wearily, her voice now slightly slurred. Agatha guessed that despite Lucy's protestations that she did not like to drink alone, she had been doing just that.

"But don't you want to find out who killed him?"

"I s'pose. It would mean I could get the hell out of here."

"Didn't you love your husband?"

"I thought I did. I was looking for money and security, and believe it or not, children. But Tolly can't make children, or so it turned out, and Tolly turned out to be a bore when we got down here and he decided his role in life was to be the squire of Fryfam. His name's Terence and he was Terry in London. But down here, he decided to be Tolly to fit in with all the tight-arses in the hunt and their stupid nick-names. I think that lot never grew out of the nursery."

Agatha's drink was very strong. "How long will it be before you can sell the house?"

"Oh, God, I don't know. I hope it's not too long. Christ, it takes a mint to run this place. Another week and I'm going to sell off the livestock. We've got sheep and cows. I've already rented out the shoot. Surely they can't stop me doing that."

"Fryfam's an odd little place," said Agatha. "I mean, first the fairies, then the murders, all these passions lying just underneath the surface."

Lucy grinned. "Talking about passion, how's the delicious Charles?"

"As usual. Just a friend."

"Might try my luck there. Is he rich?"

"I believe so, but he's the sort of man who conveniently forgets his wallet when it's time to pay the bill in a restaurant."

"Then why do you put up with him?"

"Because I'm not dependent on him."

"Oh, and are you pair detecting?"

"We're trying."

"Getting anywhere?"

"I've a feeling we're nearly there. All sorts of threads being drawn together," said Agatha sententiously. The drink *was* strong. "I think Paul Redfern knew something and I think he was going to tell the police if he didn't get paid."

"I'd better get on," said Lucy, draining her glass and putting it down.

Agatha left the remains of her own drink and got to her feet. She realized she hadn't taken off her coat and yet had not felt too warm.

"Central heating broken down?" she asked.

"Air in the pipes or something. I'll get someone in tomorrow."

Agatha walked into the hall. "Well, goodbye, Lucy," she said.

"Just don't go around sticking your nose into things or you could get hurt," said Lucy.

Agatha paused with her hand on the doorknob. "That a threat?"

"You're the sort that sees villains under the bed. Only a friendly warning."

Agatha left and walked down the long drive. She took a deep breath of air to clear her head. She went over everything Lucy had said. There wasn't much. But had she really meant poachers when she said the fools had killed Paul? Why would a townie like Lucy think of poachers? Large-scale poachers could be violent. That much she knew from the newspapers. The sort of poachers who dynamited salmon pools. But the sort who snared rabbits, maybe caught the occasional pheasant? Hardly.

She would discuss it with Charles. She wondered whether he had found out anything.

She felt suddenly hungry. The effect of the strong drinks was wearing off.

Agatha reached her cottage at last, took out her massive door key, and put it in the lock. The door was unlocked. Charles must be home. She walked in and called out, "I'm back." She saw two packets with bolts still on the table in the hall. "I see you haven't fixed those bolts yet," she shouted. "Did you get anything out of Rosie? Was Lucy having an affair?"

Her two cats came up to her, their fur erect on their backs. She stooped down and patted them. "There, now," she crooned. "What's frightened you? Where's Charles?"

And then she felt something hard shoved into her back and a man's voice said, "Into the sitting-room, Mrs. Raisin."

Agatha twisted around. Barry Jones was standing there holding a shotgun.

She walked into the sitting-room, her frightened mind racing. Mrs. Jackson was in a chair by the fireplace. "Sit down and shut up," she said.

"You!" Agatha sat down in the chair opposite.

Barry Jones stood behind the sofa, the shotgun levelled at Agatha.

"We're waiting for your friend," said Mrs. Jackson.

"Why?" demanded Agatha through white lips.

"You'll see."

"Lucy said the fools murdered Paul. That was you and your son."

"She phoned and told us she thought you were beginning to figure it out."

Agatha looked at Barry Jones, handsome Barry Jones, although he did not look handsome at that moment, with his eyes as hard as stones.

"You can't murder me and Charles," said Agatha. "You may think you can get away with two murders. But four!"

"There won't be any evidence," said Mrs. Jackson. "You'll just disappear, then we'll pack your stuff and bury it."

Agatha had a sudden desperate desire to pee. But she would not mess herself in front of these killers. She tried to forget the peril she was in and concentrate on why they had done it.

She looked again at Barry Jones, handsome Barry Jones who didn't have the money to support a woman with expensive tastes like Lucy. Unless . . .

She looked at him. "I think you were having an affair with Lucy. I think she got you to kill Tolly. Wait a bit. You, Betty Jackson, told her about that will. So she stole the Stubbs and gave it to one of you to hide. Then what? A row with Tolly? Going to change his will again and leave everything to Lizzie? Or had he found out about Lucy and Barry? Anyway, Barry here slits his throat while Lucy goes to London to get an alibi. But why then dump the Stubbs on me? If you had burnt it, say, she would have got the insurance money."

"No harm in you knowing," said Mrs. Jackson. "Lucy thought if we dumped it on you, police attention would switch to you and Lizzie. She said it was worth it. She said she'd get enough from selling the estate."

"You think you've been very clever," said Agatha, "but you can't get away with making the pair of us disappear, as you put it. Charles is a baronet and the newspapers will have a field day. The case will go on and on. Lucy will have to wait a hell of a long time for her money, which means you will, too. And you've been silly. What made you think I knew anything?"

"Lucy phoned us and said you'd figured out Paul was blackmailing us and she said you would soon work it all out and tell the police."

Agatha heard the cats patter into the hall, heard them purring and mewing. That'll be Charles, she thought. If only I could warn him. But then the cats fell silent.

Agatha clasped her hands tightly together

to stop their trembling. They were going to kill her. Was there any way she could make a dash for it?

She got to her feet. "I've got to go to the bathroom."

"Sit down!" barked Mrs. Jackson. "The only place you're going is the grave."

"You can't shoot both of us," pleaded Agatha. "The blast of the shotgun will be heard."

"Who by?" asked Barry Jones with a grin. "You're at the end of the lane. Nothing nearby except the church."

Agatha closed her eyes and prayed. Fright had made her deaf. She could only hear a roaring in her ears. Get me out of this and I'll give up smoking and I'll be a nicer person and I'll do good works. I know I haven't been very nice in the past, O Lord, but just get me out of this one and I'll be a saint. She suddenly knew she was going to pee herself and let out a low groan and opened her eyes. Then she blinked and stared again at the tableau in front of her.

The sitting-room was full of policemen. Barry Jones slowly dropped the shotgun onto the sofa. Detective Chief Inspector Hand stepped to the front as Jones and his mother were handcuffed.

"Where are you going, Mrs. Raisin?" he

shouted as Agatha began to frantically push her way through to the door of the sitting-room.

"The bathroom!" shouted Agatha and fled up the stairs.

At two o'clock the following morning, Charles and Agatha returned from police headquarters. "So that's that," said Charles, walking into the sitting-room and beginning to put fire-lighters and logs on the fire. "I couldn't believe it. You'd left the door open. I knew something was up because the cats' fur was standing on end. I backed out and took a peek into the sitting-room. I knew Hand and the police were at the pub, and we all came round."

"Yes, you've told me all that, but you haven't told me why Rosie should tell you that she knew Lucy and Barry were having an affair, that she'd once spotted them out in the woods. Why tell you when she hadn't told the police?"

"We got friendly," said Charles, his back to Agatha as he struck a match and lit the fire.

"Pillow talk?"

"You could say that."

"You are amoral," said Agatha.

"Come on, Agatha. I sussed she must

know something. You didn't think I was going to clear off for Christmas and leave you here on your own? I did it for you."

"The next thing is you'll be saying you did it for England!"

"That, too. Don't get mad at me, Aggie. Just think. The minute she told me about Barry Jones, I called on the police at the pub. Rosie was furious with me. She tried to claw my eyes out and called me a bastard."

Agatha sat down and put her hands out to the blaze. "But you weren't even going to wait to tell me first. You wanted all the glory for yourself."

"I didn't know where you were. I came back looking for you."

"I don't think I really know you, Charles."

"Who ever knows anyone?" he said lightly. "It's all solved. Just the way you told the police. So the glory is yours. Lucy worked Barry up to murdering Tolly. You're tired. Let's go to bed. You've had a bad fright."

Tired as she was, Agatha lay awake for quite a long time. James. Her mind was full of James Lacey again. He was a strong man, not a lightweight philanderer like Charles, thought Agatha, forgetting that James was just as capable of philandering as Charles. She could see James in her mind's eye — his strong face, his bright blue eyes, his tall rangy figure, his thick black hair going grey at the sides. She was suddenly desperate to get back to Carsely, to get him out of the clutches of the mysterious Mrs. Sheppard.

She was awakened at nine o'clock the following morning by Charles, shouting to her that a police car had arrived to take them to headquarters to make more statements. She hurriedly washed and dressed and went downstairs to join him, grumbling, "I feel I talked to them all of last night."

Agatha was interviewed by Chief Detective Inspector Hand. He took her all through the events of the previous day again. Then he said, "You are lucky Sir Charles had the good sense to contact us. You put yourself at grave risk by keeping information to yourself."

"I didn't *know* anything!" howled Agatha. "How could I tell you when I didn't know?"

"You nearly got killed because you told Mrs. Trumpington-James that you thought Paul Redfern was a blackmailer, which happened to be the truth."

"It only just occurred to me," said Agatha huffily. "How could I tell you anything when it only had just occurred to me?"

"Remember in the future to keep your nose out of police business."

"If we had kept our noses out of police business," snapped Agatha, "then you would still be looking for a murderer. If you want any more damn statements, you'll find me in Carsely. I'm going home."

Agatha was still raging when she was joined by Charles. "Never mind," he said, seeing her furious face. "I had a rotten time of it as well. You would think they might at least have been grateful. Let's get something to eat and then go and see Lizzie."

"Why the hell should we see Lizzie?"

"Come on, Aggie, it would be a nice thing to do."

Agatha bitched and grumbled her way through lunch about the iniquities of the ungrateful police.

Then, after lunch, as they were approaching Lizzie's flat, Agatha saw Mrs. Tite, the woman she had given twenty pounds to during her fictitious market-research survey into coffee. "Coming to see me again?" asked Mrs. Tite.

"I was actually going to call on Mrs. Findlay."

"Oh, nice little Mrs. Findlay has left."

"Do you know where she's gone?"

"She said something about going to relatives in the country."

They thanked her and walked away.

"I bet she's gone home," said Charles suddenly.

"Why on earth should she?"

"I always thought she would."

"But she'd escaped. A new life."

"She's been in chains too long," said Charles. "It's the Stockholm syndrome. The hostage gets to love the hostage taker."

"You think you're so right about everything. I bet you a fiver she hasn't gone anywhere near the captain."

"You're on."

Sure enough, at Breakham, Lizzie answered the door to them. She was wearing an apron and there was a dab of flour on one cheek. "Come into the kitchen," she said. "I'm baking for the church sale."

"Where's the captain?" asked Agatha nervously.

"Oh, somewhere round the farm."

"Why on earth did you return to him?" asked Agatha.

Lizzie bent down and took a tray of little sponge cakes out of the oven. "I knew Tommy couldn't do without me." She was wearing a pair of bright blue contact lenses and her hair was done in a soft, pretty style. "It's done him the world of good."

"So you're not going to sell the Stubbs and leave?"

"Oh, no. We're going to sell the Stubbs, yes, but the roof needs repairing and then maybe we'll go on a cruise. Do you want coffee or something? Although I'm actually very busy."

Outside, Agatha took out a five-pound note and handed it to Charles. "I still don't believe it," she said.

"They'll never go on that cruise, you know," said Charles. "He'll gradually get control of her again and there won't be a next time for Lizzie."

"Serves her right," said Agatha. "I never liked her anyway."

In Fryfam, Agatha called the estate agent and said she would be leaving in the morning and that she wanted her deposit and the remainder of the rent refunded. Mr. Bryman said the deposit could be refunded but not the remainder of the rent. But by the time Agatha, glad to vent her spleen on someone, had told him what she thought of Fryfam and its murders and that she would take him to the small-claims court, he caved in and said he would send her a cheque.

Agatha was still cross with Charles. She felt the fact that he'd taken Rosie to bed diminished her own night with him. She thought constantly of James.

That evening, Charles was asleep in front of the dying fire. Agatha decided to go down to the garden shed to get more logs.

She went into the frosty back garden. Then she stood and stared. Little multi-coloured lights were dancing around at the bottom of the garden. She thought she could hear faint laughter, which seemed to be half inside and half outside her head.

She went back inside and phoned Harriet. "Those Jackson children are up to their tricks again," she complained. "Shining lights at the bottom of my garden."

"It can't be them," said Harriet. "The children have been taken off to Mrs. Jackson's sister in Kent. Must be the fairies. I say, what do you think about Lucy being guilty after all?"

But Agatha answered automatically. She could somehow still hear that strange elfin laughter.

When she finally replaced the receiver and looked down the garden, there was nothing there.

But Agatha Raisin found she was too frightened to get any logs. She left Charles asleep in front of the dying fire and went to bed.

NINE

✝

The next day, Agatha could not bear to tell Charles about the strange lights. He would just say, if it hadn't been the Jackson children it might have been some angry villager. Agatha remembered a woman chief constable saying that a murder left everyone scarred.

And sure enough, as she was packing, the phone began to ring. Angry anonymous voices with strong local accents accused her of being an interfering busybody who had probably done the murder herself. After the third, she unplugged the phone from the wall.

Charles came downstairs, carrying his suitcases. "People ringing to congratulate us?"

"Locals ringing out for our blood."

"Why?"

"Because we got their dear, sweet Mrs.

Jackson banged up. Will you lead the way in your car Charles? I'm frightened of an ambush."

They loaded up their cars, Agatha tenderly placing the cats in their travelling boxes on the back seat.

As they emerged from Pucks Lane to circle the village green and take the road out of Fryfam, Agatha saw Rosie standing with a group of villagers. As Charles's car approached, Rosie's beautiful face became contorted with fury. She threw a half-brick straight at his car. The window on the passenger side smashed. Charles accelerated, and so did Agatha.

Soon they were speeding fast out of Fryfam. After several miles Charles pulled in at a garage. Agatha pulled in behind him.

"Are you all right?" she asked, getting out of the car and going up to inspect the damage of his.

"I was lucky I wasn't cut," said Charles.

"Here's my phone. Call the police."

"No, Rosie must feel used. She'll know that I got the police on to Barry. I'll phone up the glass-repair people when we stop for lunch. They're pretty nippy these days. I'll keep the brick as a souvenir."

"Then let's drive on," said Agatha. "I'm afraid they might come after us."

They stopped for lunch a few miles down the road. Charles phoned and ordered the glass to be repaired.

Over lunch, Agatha eyed him narrowly. "You didn't tell Rosie you loved her, or anything like that?"

"Not exactly. Stop glaring at me like that, Aggie. Who knows who's been sleeping with who in that accursed village."

"You should keep that half-brick as a reminder to keep your pants on next time."

"Oh, really? And who saved your life, you ungrateful cow?"

"I s'pose . . ." mumbled Agatha.

"Glad to be going home?"

"I am."

"James waiting for you?"

"Let's not talk about James."

"I think we should," said Charles. "Look, go and see that therapist I told you about."

"I don't need a shrink."

"When it comes to James Lacey, you need your head straightened out."

"Don't nag me. I'll think about it."

The glass repair-man came in with the papers for Charles to sign and said he'd have the window fixed in a matter of minutes.

"Time to go," said Charles at last. "I wonder if you would mind paying the bill, Aggie. I'm a bit short."

★★★

Agatha was weary by the time she turned down the winding country lane into Carsely. Somehow, she had pictured that in Carsely it would be warm and the sun would be shining, but night had already fallen and frost was glittering on the branches of the trees that spanned the road.

She turned into Lilac Lane. There were lights on in James's cottage and a suffocating feeling of excitement engulfed her. But fear of a cold reception kept her from stopping outside his cottage and rushing in to see him.

Agatha had phoned her cleaner, Doris Simpson, to warn her of her return. When she let herself in, the cottage was warm. Doris had switched on the central heating. On the kitchen table was a casserole with a note of welcome from Mrs. Bloxby.

"Why did I ever leave?" said Agatha aloud. She let the cats out of their boxes and then went out to get her suitcases.

A tall blond woman was just leaving James's cottage. This then must be Mrs. Sheppard, thought Agatha sourly. The woman came towards her. "Welcome home," she said, "You must be Agatha Raisin. I'm Melissa Sheppard."

"Pleased to meet you," said Agatha, looking anything but pleased.

"Can I give you a hand in with your luggage?"

Agatha opened her mouth to say a fierce NO, but then changed her mind. She simply had to find out how close this woman was to James.

"Very kind of you," she said instead.

Melissa Sheppard was blond, forty-something, slim but not the siren Agatha had envisaged.

"Just leave that case in the hall," said Agatha. "I'll unpack later. Coffee?"

"If it's not too much trouble."

"None at all. Come into the kitchen."

"I've just been calling on your neighbours," said Melissa. "I took him some of my sponge cakes. These bachelors don't know how to look after themselves."

"I've always found James pretty self-sufficient," said Agatha, plugging in the kettle.

"He told me you had investigated several crimes together. Too exciting! And you've been involved in another murder. 'Poor old thing,' I said to James, but he said, 'Don't worry about Agatha, she's formidable.'" And Melissa gave a throaty laugh.

"I'm suddenly very tired," said Agatha. "Do you mind if we leave coffee to another day?"

"Not at all. I'm always at James's, so we'll be seeing a lot of each other."

Agatha saw her out and then slammed the door with unnecessary force behind her.

Then she picked up the phone and dialled Charles's number. When he came on the line, she said, "What's the name of that therapist?"

The following day, Agatha walked along to the vicarage. It was as cold as Fryfam. Perhaps people damned the weather in Norfolk in the hope of consoling themselves that winter in Britain was lousier somewhere else.

Mrs. Bloxby greeted Agatha with delight. "Come in. I am dying to hear all about your adventures."

Agatha settled happily into an armchair in the vicarage sitting-room in front of the log fire. "I'll get tea," said Mrs. Bloxby.

Agatha had made an appointment with the therapist for the following week. She now dreamt of coming back to Carsely from a visit to the therapist cured of her obsession with James Lacey.

Mrs. Bloxby came in carrying a laden tea-tray. "The fruitcake's very good. It's a present from Mrs. Sheppard."

"Oh, her," said Agatha. "I met her last

night. She seems to be setting her cap at James."

Mrs. Bloxby's conscience pricked her. She should tell Agatha that James felt he was being hounded day and night by Mrs. Sheppard. But Mrs. Bloxby knew how miserable James had made Agatha in the past. She also knew that James had initially "come on" to Mrs. Sheppard, as that nasty modern phrase so well described it, and so it was his fault that she was chasing after him, but she said nothing about it, asking instead, "Now tell me all about Fryfam."

So Agatha did, and when she got to the end of her adventures, she had a sudden compulsion to tell Mrs. Bloxby about those fairy lights.

"'There are more things in Heaven and Earth, Horatio, than are dreamt of in our philosophy,'" said Mrs. Bloxby.

"Who the hell's Horatio?" demanded Agatha.

"It's a quote from Hamlet. I probably didn't get it right. I mean, that odd things do happen. On the other hand, if, as you say, some of the villagers were angry with you, then it follows they might have been trying to give you a scare."

"It could be, but it wasn't just the lights, it was that odd faint laughter. Half of it seemed to be inside my head."

"Well, don't worry about it. You're home now. Tell me about Charles. He must be very fond of you to stick by you through everything."

"I don't know what Charles thinks of me," said Agatha. "This cake is actually very good. Trust that rotten bitch to make good cakes. Yes, I think Charles gets easily bored and that's why he stayed. The murders provided a diversion for him."

"That seems a bit heartless."

"I don't really know what Charles thinks any more than I ever knew what James thought of me."

"Plenty of men around, Mrs. Raisin."

"Not for women of my age."

"Rubbish. You've been so tied up in thoughts of James, you've never really noticed anyone else."

Agatha was about to tell Mrs. Bloxby about the forthcoming visit to the therapist and then decided against it. It seemed such a weak thing to do, to go to a therapist. It would seem like admitting there was something mentally wrong with her and she couldn't cope on her own.

They talked about parish matters and then Agatha rose to take her leave.

"You are over James, aren't you?" asked

Mr. Bloxby on the doorstep.

"Oh, sure, sure," said Agatha, but she would not meet Mrs. Bloxby's eyes, and she hurried away with her head down.

Doris Simpson, her cleaner, was waiting for her when she got back. "How's my Wyckhadden cat?" asked Agatha. She had brought a cat back with her from one of her previous "cases" but had found three cats just too much and the new cat adored Doris and so Doris had taken it over.

"Happy as ever," said Doris. "Do you want me cleaning today?"

"It looks fine," said Agatha. "Leave it for a couple of days. I haven't unpacked most of my stuff yet."

The doorbell rang. "Want me to get it?" asked Doris.

"No, it's all right. Off you go and I'll see you tomorrow."

Agatha opened the door. Melissa Sheppard stood there. "Is James here?" she asked brightly. "I've made him a spinach pie."

Agatha stepped out into the front garden and looked along at James's cottage. A face glimmered at the window on the half-landing and then disappeared. "Did you ring his bell?" asked Agatha.

"Yes, but there's no reply."

I'm sure that was James at that window, thought Agatha, with a sudden burst of hope.

"Maybe he's gone out for a drive," she said.

"His car's there," Melissa pointed out.

"Oh, so it is. He usually walks down to the shop for the newspapers about this time."

"I'll try there," said Melissa and hurried off.

Agatha retreated inside. Her fingers itched to pick up the receiver and call James, but James should call her first. She could not bear a cold welcome.

She went upstairs and began to sort through the clothes in her suitcases, putting the dirty laundry into a basket.

The doorbell rang again. Agatha ran downstairs and opened the door. Her friend, Detective Sergeant Bill Wong, stood on the doorstep. "I wondered whether you would come back alive," he said.

"Come in. Have coffee. Hear all about it," said Agatha. "In fact, it's nearly lunch-time. I haven't done any shopping yet. But I'm sure I've something in the freezer I can put in the microwave."

"I can't stay very long," said Bill. "That Detective Chief Inspector Hand doesn't like you at all."

"Why, we solved his case for him."

"He swears they had already arrived at the same conclusion, so there was no need to put yourself at risk."

"Well, he's got to say that, hasn't he? To cover up his incompetence."

"Could be. So tell me all about it."

Bill was amused by Agatha's flat and factual account. The old Agatha would have bragged and told a highly embroidered story. He did not know that most of Agatha's mind was on James.

"Anyway, I'd better get back on duty," he said. "It's good to have you back. We'll maybe have dinner next week?"

"Lovely. Give me a ring."

Agatha waved him goodbye and then carried her dirty laundry down to the washing machine in the kitchen. Again the doorbell went. She was half inclined not to answer it. But she went and opened the door.

James Lacey stood there, looking down at her.

Agatha blinked. She had imagined him there so many times that at first she thought if she blinked very hard he would disappear and the figure would reappear as someone ordinary, like the postman.

"Any chance of coffee, Agatha?" asked James. "Have you something in your eye?"

"No, I'm fine. Come in. Melissa's looking for you."

"Oh, that tiresome woman."

"Could you put the kettle on, James? I'm going upstairs for a minute."

Agatha dived into her bedroom and made up her face carefully and brushed her thick hair until it shone.

Then she went downstairs. James was standing with his back to her, spooning coffee into two mugs.

He turned round. Oh, that smile! "So what's all this murder and mayhem you've been involved in?"

So Agatha sat down and told her story again.

James handed her a mug of coffee and then sat down opposite her and stretched out his long legs. When she had finished, he said, "You and Charles seem to be close."

"Oh, no," protested Agatha. "Just friends."

"You weren't just friends in Cyprus."

"That was a one-off," said Agatha, blushing. "I was upset and you were being so awful to me." She felt suddenly miserable. James looked angry. Soon he would get up and walk out and that would be that.

"I wanted to go over to Norfolk, but Mrs. Bloxby told me that you and Charles were an item."

"She wouldn't say that!" Agatha looked amazed. "She couldn't have said that. Not Mrs. Bloxby!"

"Come to think of it, she just implied it."

"There's nothing there and never will be. What's it to you, anyway?"

"I planned to take you out for a romantic dinner and say this, but what the hell, here goes. Agatha Raisin, will you marry me?"

Agatha clutched at the kitchen table for support. "Have I heard you properly? Do you want to marry me?"

"Yes."

"Why?"

He looked irritated. "Because life is very dull without you and I have bores like Melissa preying on me."

The little bit of common sense that was left in Agatha's mind was shouting to her that he had not said anything about love. She ignored it.

"Yes, okay," she said. "When?"

"After Christmas. January sometime. I'll run over to the registry office in Mircester and fix things up."

"Don't you want a church wedding?" asked Agatha.

"Not really."

"Oh, all right, then."

James got to his feet. "I'll pick you up for dinner at eight."

"Yes."

He kissed the top of her head and left.

Agatha sat in a daze.

After all the waiting and longing, here it was at last. She had to tell someone. The doorbell went again.

Melissa Sheppard stood there, again. "Someone told me that James came in here," she said.

"Yes, he was here." Happiness lit up Agatha's face. "We're going to be married."

"What! That's not possible."

"Why, may I ask?"

"He's been sleeping with me."

"Just go away!" Agatha banged the door in her face. Her hands were trembling. No, she would not confront James about Melissa. He was marrying Agatha Raisin and that was that. Nothing and no one was going to stop that. She tried to settle down to house-keeping but found she could not. She phoned Charles.

"I'm going to cancel that therapist," she said. "James and I are getting married."

"Mistake, darling. He'll try to turn you into a Lizzie and he won't be able to, so the pair of you will fight like cat and dog."

"Rubbish. I've a good mind not to invite

you to the wedding."

"I wouldn't miss it for worlds. I like a good funeral."

Fuming, Agatha hung up on him. Then she thought, Mrs. Bloxby, dear Mrs. Bloxby would wish her well.

She put on her coat and marched off to the vicarage. "What's the matter?" asked Mrs. Bloxby, opening the door to her. "You look upset. Come in."

"I'm the happiest woman in the world," said Agatha firmly.

"Why is that?"

"James and I are getting married."

"Oh, Agatha Raisin, you *fool*."

"What do you mean?"

"It'll end in disaster. Oh, he's nice enough, I grant you, but when it comes to women, he's cold and selfish. He had a fling with Mrs. Sheppard and then decided she bored him to death. I beg you, don't accept him."

"I thought you were my friend," shrieked Agatha. "Damn the lot of you. I'm marrying James Lacey and no one is going to stop me."

And no one did. Agatha Raisin and James Lacey were married on a cold January day in Mircester Registry Office. The bride wore a smart honey-coloured wool suit and a dashing hat. There was to be no reception. She and James were leaving immediately to honeymoon in Vienna.

The "funeral," as Sir Charles Fraith called it, was held at the vicarage, Mrs. Bloxby having invited several of Agatha's friends back for a buffet lunch.

"Poor Mrs. Raisin," sighed Mrs. Bloxby. "I'm surprised she even invited any of us harbingers of doom."

"She didn't look at all happy," said Roy Silver, a public relations man who had once worked for Agatha.

"I think he's a bit of a bully. Agatha's kept her cottage, you know," said Doris Simpson, "and she was doing his washing and he came in and started raging because she hadn't separated his whites from his coloureds."

"If anyone can cut him down to size, it'll be our Aggie," said Roy.

Charles helped himself to a piece of cake. "I think she'll murder him."

There was a shocked silence.

"Just joking," said Charles. "This cake is jolly good."